THE FINAL TRAIL

by A.A. Abbott

Published by Perfect City Press.

This book was written by a British writer in British English.

ISBN 978-1-913395-00-1

A FEW WORDS OF THANKS

Thanks to my editor, Katharine D'Souza, and everyone else who helped me make this book great, especially:

Ali AElsey
Carolyn Stubbs
Cathy Fagg
Chris Hills
Colin Ward
David Rigby
David Wake
Dawn Brookes
Dennis Zaslona
Garry Hyde
Helen Combe
James Wilson
Jean Burnett
Jeremy White
Jo Ullah
Katherine Evans
Lee Benson
Michèle Weibel
Michelle Armitage
Nicola Armstrong
Nigel Howl
Patricia Gregory
Paula Good
Pete Crawford
Sarah Spilsbury
Suzanne Ferris
Suzanne McConaghy
Tiffany Elliott
Tracey Preater

I really appreciate your help!

A.A. Abbott

BY A.A. ABBOTT

Up In Smoke

After The Interview

The Bride's Trail

The Vodka Trail

The Grass Trail

The Revenge Trail

The Final Trail

*See **aaabbott.co.uk** for my blog, free short stories and more.*
Sign up for my newsletter to receive news, freebies and offers.

*Follow me on Twitter **@AAAbbottStories** and **Facebook**.*

Contents

Chapter 1.   Kat

"I opened the door," Kat said, "and saw a man with a gun."

She heard muffled gasps from the public gallery behind her. Shaun Halloran's inquest had attracted quite an audience. The London gangster had died at his son's hand over a year before, but Kat's involvement lent the case a touch of glamour. Media, family, friends and random onlookers were squashed into the oak benches. Despite the unseasonal April heat, barely disturbed by a brass fan whirring overhead, the courtroom's atmosphere was charged with excitement.

To her right, the jurors' eyes bored into her. Before, they'd been slouching in their casual outfits, layers gradually removed as the humid air took hold. Now, Kat had their full attention. There was even a slack-jawed stare from the young, bearded man who'd been leering when she took the stand earlier.

She was hardly dressed to thrill. Her plain black shift and jacket was a frumpy choice for a twenty-seven-year-old. It didn't flatter her curves like the outfits she'd worn for glossy magazine shoots, but it contrasted with her blonde hair and creamy skin. A lapel brooch highlighted her green eyes.

Amy, her best friend, had counselled Kat on her appearance before they packed for the trip to London. Kat was well-known as the face of Starshine vodka, the craft brand that was the trendiest drink this year. There would be media interest. She needed to look smart.

Knowing Amy was sitting behind the witness box, only inches away, gave Kat strength to face the jury. Even so, she was gripping the edge of the wooden witness box to stop her hands shaking. The only way she'd coped with the events of that day was to keep memories buried.

To the left of the jury, the coroner, Dr Henry Micklegate, directed proceedings. Although he wore a business suit rather than judge's robes, his status was emphasised by being raised above everyone else. His carved oak chair, adorned with the royal coat of arms like the window behind it, stood on a dais. A table before him hosted ring binders and documents. He scrutinised these before peering at Kat through frameless spectacles.

"I'm sure we all know the answer," Micklegate said, "but nevertheless, I must ask you, Miss White – did you know the man?" His voice was a monotone, neat and clipped as his thinning white hair.

"Yes," Kat said. "It was Shaun Halloran." He should have been in prison. She'd given evidence against him: seen him sentenced to life for murder. Her biggest regret was standing, paralysed with shock, when she should have slammed that door.

Micklegate's words cut through her self-recrimination. "Thank you. Tell us what happened next."

"He punched me, here." She indicated the left side of her head, above the ear. "I stumbled, but managed to right myself. Then he asked where the bedroom was."

This time, it was as if everyone in the public gallery inhaled simultaneously.

"No." The cry of outrage was Tim's.

Kat's fiancé had insisted on joining her for the inquest to give his support. He hadn't heard all these details before, though. How could he, when the last thing she wanted to do was reprise them?

Micklegate scowled, flashing a silent warning over her shoulder. He said nothing to Tim, however, sympathy now evident in his tone as he asked Kat, "What did you do?"

"I kneed him in the balls, and tried to scratch his eyes out," Kat said.

She trembled, remembering how she'd fought for her life. With nothing to lose, she'd used every ounce of her strength and ingenuity. Whatever he'd planned to do first, Shaun was always going to kill her. She'd known that from the second she'd seen him at the upmarket hotel.

"He didn't shoot me." Shaun had been far too calculating for that. "Instead, he thumped my stomach, and," she pointed lower down her abdomen, "here. The pain was so intense, I couldn't move.

"Then Dee came downstairs, in her wedding dress. There was a living room above the suite's lobby, and we'd been relaxing there before the ceremony."

"That was to take place elsewhere in the building, wasn't it?" Micklegate asked, apparently keen to move the narrative forward.

"Yes. Dee thought our visitor was Marshall Jenner, one of her friends. Of course, it wasn't." How could Kat describe the fear on Dee's face, when she saw an escaped murderer brandishing a pistol? "Shaun pointed the gun at Dee, and said he'd kill her if I didn't do exactly what I was told. So, I gave in."

Kat had steeled herself for death, trying to disconnect from whatever Shaun did before it happened. She hadn't reckoned on her friend.

"But I threw up," she said. "I couldn't help it after the walloping he gave me. I was pregnant at the time. I'm sure that's when my miscarriage started." Tears welled as she pictured Tim behind her now, hearing how his child had died. Unlike Kat, he'd been thrilled about their unplanned baby. It was only the loss that had made her realise, too late, the love she felt towards this tiny, wondrous being.

Despite the passage of time, grief still clung to her. Perhaps it always would.

Micklegate's voice softened again. "Would you like a short break to compose yourself, Miss White?"

"No. I want to finish this." Kat sniffed. Giving her testimony was harder than she'd envisaged, but she must endure it.

Micklegate's clerk, a young woman, handed Kat a box of tissues.

She took one gratefully, dabbing at her eyes. "I lost the baby, but that was later. When I was sick, it distracted Shaun. Not for long, but enough that Dee had a chance to attack him. She was very brave. Once she started grappling with him, he lost control of the gun. He couldn't see well enough to shoot us, but he struck me across the face with it. Then his son arrived."

"Tell me more about that."

"I felt dizzy and began to fall. As I hit the floor, Shaun opened the door of the suite. Ben was there."

"Did you know him?"

"No. I'd met him once, when he tried to chat up my friend in a bar." Amy shouldn't have engaged in conversation with Ben, but everyone made mistakes. "I had no idea who he was. Shaun gave it away. 'Shoot those crazy bitches, son,' he said."

"What did Ben Halloran do?"

"I can't say. I only saw his eyes before I fainted." Blue, dark-fringed and troubled like Shaun's, she'd believed their presence presaged her death. Dee couldn't possibly fend off two killers. "When I awoke, I was with a paramedic and a policeman."

"Did you see Shaun or Ben Halloran again?"

"No. I was sent to hospital, thankful to be alive." She had been wracked with agony, though, both physical and mental. There were bruises all over her body, while the miscarriage, and the searing guilt it brought, had just begun.

"Thank you, Miss White. I have no further questions for you. As I explained before, others may. First, we'll invite Ben Halloran's lawyer to raise any queries he may have. Mr Curtis?"

Curtis, a slight, balding figure in a grey suit, was sitting alone at a long, low table in front of the coroner. He shook his head.

"Thank you, Mr Curtis. Members of the jury, do you wish to ask Miss White anything?"

Kat stood frozen in her wooden pen, willing them to be silent.

The man with the beard raised his hand. He was scruffy, with straggly dark hair, dressed in a black leather jacket and T-shirt sporting an anarchist symbol.

Micklegate nodded to him.

"How did you know Shaun and Ben Halloran?" the juror asked. He was grinning, enjoying his moment in the spotlight. "Were they your lovers?"

The oak-panelled courtroom began to spin around her. Kat clung to the sides of the witness box, steadying herself.

She was about to explain that nothing could be further from the truth, when Micklegate said, "That question isn't relevant. You needn't say more, Miss White. Does anyone have a different query?"

The firmness of his tone deterred the rest of the jury, as well as Kat's inquisitor.

"No?" Dr Micklegate raised an eyebrow. "In that case, I see no need to detain our witness any longer. Miss White, you may go."

She wanted to run from the chamber, from the court processes, well-meaning friends and blistering memories. Instead, her legs wobbled. To her relief, Kat made it to the oak doors opposite the jury, without a backward glance.

She passed into a lobby: small, dark and claustrophobic. The stuffy air seemed to suck breath from her lungs. It emerged in short, sharp gasps until, like a diver resurfacing, she burst from the tiny room onto a light and bright landing. A stone staircase led to the building's imposing entrance on the floor below. Freedom and sunshine lay within her grasp.

She hadn't quite reached the first step when she heard doors swishing open.

"Kat, wait," Tim called.

She couldn't bear to look.

His voice was lost in the clamour, as journalists surged towards her, tugging at her sleeve.

"Miss White, how are you feeling?"

"Was Shaun your boyfriend?"

"Kat, darling, I can offer you an exclusive – my paper will pay good money…"

She pulled away from the press pack, biting her lip. Tears nevertheless flowed freely. Attempting to dry her eyes with the back of her hand, Kat dashed downstairs and out onto the street below.

The reporters followed. Mobile phones and microphones were thrust in her face; cameras flashed.

"I can't speak now," she whispered. Outside, the air, laden with exhaust fumes, seemed even more stifling than in the courtroom. Sweat prickled her skin and dampened her hair into curls. She removed the uncomfortable black jacket.

Amy pushed through the crowd. "You left your bag," she said, thrusting the cheap satchel into Kat's hands.

"Thanks." Kat looked down, unable to meet her friend's eyes. There was no way she was talking to Tim, journalists or anyone else, either. Panic threatened to overwhelm her if she couldn't escape.

A red bus slowed to a halt, mere yards away. She made as if to catch it, then raced past the queue, rushing around the rear of the vehicle and across the busy street.

Heedless of high heels pinching, Kat ran until she saw a black cab for hire. She hailed it, barely noticing Amy and Tim's shocked faces among the throng as the taxi left them behind.

Tim would have even more questions. She couldn't deal with them. It was bad enough casting her mind back to the horror of that final encounter with Shaun.

She'd read Shaun wrong when they first met. Although she knew he was a villain, she thought she could handle him. Now, she had a job she loved, making vodka, but her circumstances had been very different three years before. As a croupier in London's West End, she'd lived in a flat she could barely afford and drifted from party to party without a purpose.

The promise of cash had blinded her when Shaun asked her to train the croupiers in his speakeasy.

That had gone pear-shaped when he thought she'd stolen from him. Even though it wasn't true, it had led to his arrest and life imprisonment. She'd testified against him, having seen him kill a man as easily as lighting a cigarette.

Forgiveness wasn't his style. She knew why he'd come to that hotel room.

Shaun's death had freed her from his menace. He couldn't reach her from the grave.

But his sons were still alive.

Chapter 2.   Ben

At an early age, Ben Halloran's father had impressed on him that he should look smart in court.

"They're all posh," Shaun had said. "Your brief, the Crown's brief, the judge or magistrate. They mingle with lawyers and other rich wasters with more money than sense. They'll wear fine suits, and you should too. You want to seem as good as them. Get kitted out in Savile Row. And speak properly. No dropping your aitches. Don't swear, either. Juries don't like it."

It hadn't occurred to Shaun, counselling his young son, that Ben would grow up without the slightest desire to break the law. Ben ignored his father's sartorial advice too. When he arrived at Shaun's inquest, he was clad in a navy T-shirt and jeans.

It was the most practical choice for a trip on the Tube in hot weather, and the Tube was the quickest mode of travel, but today he hated it. Jammed upright in a rush hour carriage, he smelled sweat, bad breath and cheap aftershave. Perspiration plastered his floppy brown fringe to his forehead. Ben staggered onto the platform at his destination, desperate for another shower. He should have suffered the pain of an earlier alarm call and travelled by cab with Neil Curtis. The lawyer had suggested it.

Instead, they were meeting at Prêt à Manger. Ben headed for a road junction where glassy office skyscrapers abruptly gave way to an enclave of lower rise red brick mansion flats. Neil was waiting in the busy café.

Air-conditioning delivered an icy blast as Ben walked inside. Neil, sitting at the back, pointed to two cardboard cups.

"I bought you a coffee. Want anything else?" The lawyer's voice was quiet and bland, like his appearance.

"No, thanks."

"Sit down, and let's have a quick recap on what you can expect. Miss Saxton will give evidence first, then it'll be you – probably after lunch."

"She spoke up for me to the police."

"Yes, thanks to her you weren't prosecuted, but the CPS may change their minds if she tells a different tale today."

"Why would she?" A chill surged down the nape of Ben's neck. It wasn't the aircon.

"Why indeed? If she casts you in a bad light, rest assured I'll push back. Meanwhile, stick to your story. It was self-defence, all right?"

"That's the truth. But suppose they don't believe me? What then?"

"Let's cross that bridge if we have to." Neil's pale grey eyes were unreadable.

"Would I go to prison?"

"If you're charged, and I emphasise, if, I will apply for bail. It's not always granted for a serious offence like murder, but I think you'd get it. You'd almost certainly have to surrender your passport, though."

"So I couldn't go abroad?" Without the ability to travel to gaming conventions outside the UK, Ben's eSports career would be severely limited. The big money was in sponsorship deals and prize tournaments overseas.

It could be far worse, of course: if found guilty, he'd be jailed. Ben didn't even want to think about that.

Neil's expression remained neutral. "Don't panic. The CPS will do nothing unless the inquest verdict is one of unlawful killing. Even then, you may not be charged – the Crown would have to build a case. My advice to you is to keep it simple today. Say as little as possible. You could face questions from the coroner and the jury – all eleven of them. There's no need to answer if you think it's a trap."

"Aren't there twelve people on the jury?"

"Not in a coroner's court. Also, be aware there's an outside chance your younger brother will be brought along from Belmarsh prison. He was expected yesterday, but he didn't turn up. If he does, he can question you as well. Think you can cope?"

Ben nodded. If Jon appeared, there was a chance of reconciliation. "Can I talk to him?"

"Not privately, I'm afraid." Neil glanced at his watch. "We'd better go."

The coroner's court was housed in a handsome double-fronted brick building with a stone portico. In keeping with its surroundings, it was about a century old and three storeys high. Half a dozen reporters and photographers were clustered around the entrance.

Microphones were thrust towards Ben as he arrived.

"What do you think of Kat White's testimony?"

"Did you shoot to kill?"

"We're making no comment, either now or later." Neil Curtis clapped an arm around Ben's shoulder.

It felt odd, as the older man was six inches shorter. Ben allowed himself to be guided past the media, thinking this was how a cornered animal must feel, trapped by baying wolves. He was used to sycophantic gaming journalists rather than these bloodthirsty creatures.

Twin maroon doors, each decorated with a gold-painted portcullis, were set into the porch. They were locked. Neil pressed the intercom button. A hiss of static signalled someone was listening.

"We're here for Shaun Halloran's inquest," the lawyer said.

"Press will be admitted soon. Twenty past nine at the latest." It was a woman's voice, well-spoken.

"I'm a lawyer and I'm here with my client. He's a witness: Ben Halloran."

"Why didn't you say so?"

A minute later, a young woman peeped out through the door. Braided brown hair topped a black skirt suit and white shirt. Her grooming was of air hostess standard. "Come on in," she said, noticeably friendlier.

The interior was grand in a stuffy, old-fashioned way, painted white with dark polished wood in evidence. There was a plush red carpet. Ben decided not to remark on it. Appearing at his father's inquest wasn't the celebrity he craved.

The girl pointed to a stone staircase, balustraded in oak and wrought iron. "I'll show you to the courtroom."

"I know the way," Neil told her.

Disappointed, Ben watched as she disappeared down a corridor, hips swaying in her tight skirt. He followed Neil up the steps.

The first floor courtroom, square and wood-panelled, was as stately as its environs. Neil indicated the coroner's throne-like chair, a brass sign before it revealing he was called Dr Henry Micklegate; the jury benches; and the witness box. "I'll sit at that table, near the coroner. You take a pew in the public gallery."

The rows of benches did indeed resemble a church's pews. Ben scanned them.

"Uncle Clive!"

His father's cousin was lounging by a window at the rear. On the sill beside him, a brass plate announced 'PRESS'. Clive, a panel beater, had taken no notice of it. He ignored Ben, too.

15

Ben waved. He'd always clicked with Clive, who was only a decade older. They'd shared PlayStation games when Ben was small. Ben thought fondly that it had been the start of his journey to making a living from eSports.

Clive didn't acknowledge the greeting. He stared at the ceiling, his muscled, tattooed arms folded across his West Ham-shirted chest.

"Ben." The soft female voice brought a pang of recognition. She was in the second row, a twenty-something girl, hair falling messily in copper waves over a navy jacket.

"Amy." Relieved to see a friendly face, he slipped into the space beside her, at the edge of a central aisle. He was pleased he'd remembered her name. If only he could recall when they'd met. There was an attractive geekiness about her, but he was sure she wasn't one of his gaming fangirls.

She fixed her gaze on his, and the memory returned. He'd tried to chat her up in a cocktail bar. She'd been drinking with Kat White, whose evidence had put his father in jail – Kat White, whose presence at a society wedding had drawn Shaun Halloran to central London with murder on his mind.

Ben hadn't known who they were when he'd approached Amy then. For an instant, he longed for those innocent times, before he had blood on his hands.

"I'm sorry," he gabbled, before she could look away. "About your friend, and my father…"

"Don't. You tried to help." Amy frowned, but her voice was amicable. He hadn't managed to take her telephone number before. This morning, he decided, he had a second chance.

"Why are you here?" he asked. Was it to see him? His rising hope fell away. Amy was Kat's friend, of course, and must be supporting her. Still, he couldn't see Kat's blonde head anywhere.

Amy gestured to the couple next to her.

Like Neil Curtis, they came from a different generation. Ben's eyes would normally flick across them and move on. The man, his dark mane waxed and flashed with grey, wore a sober charcoal suit. His caramel-haired companion was less restrained, her short scarlet dress revealing long legs. Ben thought they must be Amy's parents. As they turned towards him, smiles beginning and rapidly vanishing, he realised he was half right. This was Amy's father and her stepmother-to-be: Dee, the bride that Shaun had tried to kill.

Ben could tell she didn't wish to engage. Trying to avoid Dee's accusing glare, he pretended to switch off his phone. Blood pounded in his temples.

The door swung open to admit several journalists, who headed for the press area at the back. They were followed by a motley crowd, most of whom filed onto the jurors' benches. Only a white-haired man, and the girl who had admitted Ben earlier, remained.

"The court will rise," she said.

Everyone else stood. Ben copied them.

"Good morning," the man said. "Please sit down." Bespectacled and neat in a suit, it was obvious who he was. He slid onto his elaborately carved chair. "We're resuming the inquest into the death of Shaun Michael Halloran. We have a potentially interested person joining us. For the benefit of those who don't know, PIPs are close relatives of the deceased. They may question witnesses at the inquest, and I understand this is likely to be the case today. To accommodate him, we need three seats at the front, which I see we have." He signalled to three bentwood chairs beside Neil Curtis.

"Must be Jonathan Halloran," a gruff voice whispered from the press benches.

Ben craned his neck as the door opened. He looked straight into his brother's eyes.

They were light blue, hard and angry. Although barely an adult, and manacled between two prison officers, twenty-year-old Jon projected an aura of power.

Without blinking, Jon unleashed a gobbet of spittle in Ben's direction. Ben ducked, needlessly. The slick of foam fell short, landing on the parquet floor.

"That's enough, Halloran," one of the prison officers snarled. "You're on basic regime as soon as we're back."

"Tell me how. Just for coughing?" Jon challenged, with the look of a man who had read the prison rulebook back to front and sideways. His Adam's apple wobbled beneath his pale skin.

"Mr Halloran!" Micklegate had noticed the commotion. "You have a right to attend this inquest, but on the basis that you observe its rules. One of these is adherence to rudimentary standards of courtesy. Is that understood?"

Slowly, his lips set in a truculent line, Jon nodded.

"Thank you." Micklegate waited until Jon and his companions were settled before him, then continued. "We heard yesterday from Miss Arad, who conducted the post-mortem, from Sergeant Lucas, who was the first policeman to arrive at the scene, and from Miss White."

Jon jumped to his feet, with enough force to drag both his escorts with him. "I would have questioned them, if I'd been here. I have a right."

"I apologise, Mr Halloran," Micklegate said. "You do have that right. There appears to have been some mix-up within the prison service. However, during my questioning, I suspect I covered any queries you might have had. Would you like to see the transcripts? We can adjourn for twenty minutes while you read them if you like."

"I suppose so," Jon said testily.

"Fancy a quick coffee across the road?" One of the reporters touched Ben's elbow.

"Sorry, got to check my phone." Ben might have gone for coffee with Amy, but it was unwise to ask her in front of her disapproving family. In any case, it was akin to making a date inside a goldfish bowl.

He played Candy Crush to blot out the bustle of the courtroom, looking up occasionally to see his brother's puzzled expression as he flicked through the document he'd been given. It was unlikely Jon understood the dense pages of legalese, but he wasn't admitting it.

Eventually, Jon said he was satisfied. Micklegate began the day's proceedings by asking Dee to come forward.

Every man in the room ogled her legs when she wiggled past, high red stilettos click-clacking on the polished parquet. She stood patiently in the witness box, facing coroner and jury. Meanwhile, the public gallery enjoyed a view of the tight dress clinging to her bottom.

"You are Deirdre Annabel Saxton?"

"Yes." Dee's voice was throaty and warm.

"I must ask you either to swear on the Bible or affirm that the evidence you give shall be the truth, the whole truth, and nothing but the truth."

"I will affirm." She took the oath.

"Thank you, Miss Saxton. Tell me how you came to meet Shaun Halloran."

Dee sounded confused. "Meet him? Our first and only encounter was the day of his death."

"Carry on."

"It was my wedding day. Everything was ready – my dress, make-up and photos. I was waiting in my hotel suite for the bridesmaids and page boy to return. Then I was going to make my grand entrance."

"Were you alone?"

"Apart from Kat, yes. She answered the door. We were expecting a visitor: the husband of one of my friends. I went downstairs to the lobby of my suite, to find Kat fighting a gunman."

"Not the husband of one of your friends?"

"No. It turned out to be Shaun Halloran. He was beating Kat up badly, punching her in the stomach. She was pregnant."

Ben winced. For a split-second, he hated his father.

"Kat vomited – all over him, actually," Dee said. "It shocked him. All of a sudden, I realised he wasn't looking in my direction. So I jumped on top of him, and wouldn't let go. I was squeezing his torso and biting his nose. I hoped he'd drop the gun."

"And did he?"

"No, he gave it to his son. Shaun Halloran stuck a knife in my back instead."

"I gather we are lucky this is not an inquest into your death."

"Yes." Dee's tone was solemn. "I lost a lot of blood."

"The event and its memories are obviously painful, Miss Saxton, but please bear with me," Micklegate said. "How did Shaun's son gain access to the room? Was the door open?"

"No. Shaun let him in. He was banging on the door. Shaun recognised his voice."

"And did you know this was Benjamin Halloran?"

"Not then." Dee hesitated, then added, "Later, he phoned for an ambulance. That's when I heard his name."

"And you say Shaun gave the gun to Benjamin?"

"Yes. He thought his son would help him."

"Oh? What actually happened?"

The court was silent. Ben listened intently. Dee had persuaded the police that he was innocent of wrongdoing. Did she still believe that? What was she about to say?

"Shaun's son waved the gun around. He threatened to shoot everyone." Dee turned to glance at Ben. Her lips tightened. "I begged him to call an ambulance, but he ignored me."

He'd had no choice, Ben thought. How could he risk putting the gun down? His father would have seized it in an instant. Shaun wouldn't have let him ring the emergency services then.

Micklegate interrupted Dee's flow. "In your written statement, you say Benjamin's words at that point were 'All of you, stop fighting, or I will shoot.' Is that correct?"

"Yes." Dee continued, her face drawn beneath the tan. "Shaun wasn't happy about that. He attacked Benjamin. They grappled for possession of the gun. I heard a single shot, then Shaun collapsed on top of his son."

"Murderer! You killed him, Ben." Jon, his face flushed, was on his feet again. So were the two prison officers, whether voluntarily or not.

"Mr Halloran." The ice was clearly audible. "You will have an opportunity to question the witness later, but only if you can show this courtroom you can behave. This is your last chance. One more strike, and you're out. Understand?"

"Yes." Jon's shoulders slumped. He returned to his seat.

"What were you doing at this time, Miss Saxton?" Micklegate asked.

"Seriously?" Dee appeared incredulous. "Thinking of all the people I loved, of all my reasons to live, as I lost blood and my life slipped away. I heard the shot, and Benjamin crying. With what felt like my last breath, I urged him once again to call an ambulance. This time, he did."

"Thank you. I have no further questions," the coroner said. "Wait a moment, please." He inclined his head towards Jon. "Do you wish to ask Miss Saxton anything, Mr Halloran?"

"No," Jon said, to Ben's surprise.

"Thank you. There is another PIP here, of course, and that's Mr Benjamin Halloran. Mr Curtis, do you or your client have queries for Miss Saxton?"

Neil Curtis caught Ben's eye.

Ben shook his head.

"One question, if I may," Neil said, rising to his feet. His tone was unctuous. "Forgive me, Miss Saxton, I can see these are distressing recollections. I am asking you this only because of the serious impact it could have on my client's life. He is a young man of twenty-five…"

"Can you get to the point, Mr Curtis? I am not keen to detain the witness," Micklegate said.

"Of course. You mentioned, Miss Saxton, that Shaun Halloran attacked his son, Ben, and they were grappling for possession of the gun. Was the shot fired accidentally, in your view?"

"It happened so fast, I didn't see it," Dee said. "My intuition was that Benjamin didn't intend to kill his father. I already told the police that."

"So I understand," Neil said, smoothly. "Thank you for telling us, too. I have nothing else to ask of you."

"Very good," Micklegate said. "How about members of the jury?"

No one raised a hand.

"Thank you, Miss Saxton," Micklegate said. "I'd now like to call my final witness, Ben Halloran."

Dee's entourage left as Ben entered the witness box. Watching Amy disappear from view, he felt a pang of regret. It was dwarfed both by his trepidation about the jury's verdict and the bitter knowledge that his brother hated him.

He was merely inches from Jon, so close he could have ruffled that cropped dark hair. There was no chance of it. The doll-sized baby his mother had brought home from hospital; the child playing football; even the teenager who had joined him in all-night computer games – all were gone. The youth who remained was a stranger.

The stuffy air crackled with tension.

"You are Benjamin Michael Halloran?"

"Yes." Before he could be asked, Ben said, "I will swear on the Bible."

He had been brought up a Roman Catholic. When he was small, his mother had sent him to Sunday school. He'd enjoyed the Bible stories, in which the wise and the good triumphed while the bad guys burned in hell. Real life had proved more complicated.

The clerk handed Ben the book.

Ben clutched it in his right hand. "I swear by Almighty God that the evidence I shall give shall be the truth, the whole truth, and nothing but the truth."

"Thank you," Micklegate said. "Mr Curtis has no doubt explained to you that you must tell the truth under oath, but you are not obliged to answer any questions if you feel you might incriminate yourself?"

"I understand that. I will tell you anything you wish to know." Ben hoped his voice was firm and clear.

"Good. Can you tell us, then, why you went to Dee Saxton's hotel room on the twenty-second of March?"

"To see my father," Ben said. "He'd phoned me. It came out of the blue. He was supposed to be in prison."

Jon fidgeted. A glance from the coroner quelled his mutiny.

Ben brushed his fringe from his eyes. "My father told me he had a gun, and he was going to kill Kat White. I had to do some detective work to establish where they were."

"Do explain."

"I googled Kat White, and discovered she'd be at the wedding, so that's where I went."

"So you arrived, and went to Miss Saxton's hotel room," Micklegate said. "Did you have a gun?"

"No. My father gave me his. I have nothing to add to Dee Saxton's testimony."

"With respect, I think you do." There was a light beading of sweat on Micklegate's dry, papery skin. "We were told yesterday the gun was a Glock 17 pistol. I believe the model has no safety catch. Is that correct?"

"Yes."

"You are familiar with guns?"

"Only from computer games."

"So. There was no safety catch. However, to shoot, you would have to pull the trigger deliberately. You are presumably aware, from computer games, war films and whatever else that firing a bullet at someone could kill them. Why did you shoot your father?"

"Self-defence," Ben said. "I didn't want to kill him, but I had to keep the gun from him. If he'd got it back, the two women were dead meat, and I was, too."

"Are you sure? Remember, you are under oath."

"Completely sure."

"I have no more questions."

"I have." Jon sprang to his feet once more, his angular face seething with hatred.

"Very good. It is your right to ask them, Mr Halloran," Micklegate said. "You may stand if you wish."

22

Jon did so, forcing his escorts to do likewise. He turned to face Ben, a sneer giving a demonic cast to his pale features.

"Just for the record," Micklegate said, "can you confirm you are Jonathan Matthew Halloran?"

"Yes." Jon glowered, without looking at the coroner. He had eyes for one man alone. "Admit it." He cast the words at Ben like stones. "You murdered him."

A kernel of guilt twisted through Ben's mind. He forced himself to meet Jon's hostile gaze. "It was self-defence."

"No," Jon said. "It was a trap. You sprang him from the nick deliberately, so you could hunt him down and kill him."

"I didn't want Dad or anyone else to die."

"Who says? Why should I listen to you, or that tart?" Jon jerked a thumb at the door through which Dee had exited. "It was a set-up from the beginning, because he preferred me over you. He knew you were a waste of space. Everyone knows."

"I loved Dad." For the first time in the courtroom, Ben's voice shook. He reddened, recognising the truth that his father had had little time for him. They'd never understood each other, while Shaun and Jon were kindred spirits. That wasn't a basis for murder, though.

"Really," Micklegate said, "this is not intended to be an opportunity to make unsubstantiated allegations, Mr Halloran, but to ask further questions. Do you have any?"

"Just one," Jon said, glaring at the coroner. "Why don't you shut up?" He spat at Ben again, this time hitting him full in the eye.

"Take him away," Micklegate ordered the prison officers. "I will be making a complaint to your governor, and I hope he will find a way of teaching Jonathan Halloran some manners." He turned to Ben. "My clerk will get you a tissue. I apologise. It was an error of judgement on my part to allow your brother to stay."

Cursing, Jon clomped out of the room with the luckless officers.

Micklegate addressed the court. "The jury may have questions for Ben Halloran, but they can be raised after lunch. We shall break at this juncture. Mr Halloran, until then, you are not to discuss this hearing or your evidence with anyone except Mr Curtis. Understood?"

"Yes."

"Good. I'll see you all in an hour."

Neil Curtis smiled at Ben. "Ready to run the gauntlet?"

Ben winced in assent. Despite standing beneath the busily humming ceiling fan, he needed fresh air.

"I'll be outside the gents." Neil handed him a supermarket carrier bag.

Ben had no time to speculate about its contents. He left the room swiftly, glad to have a head start on the reporters. Diving into a toilet cubicle, he found a pair of sunglasses and an orange hi-vis jerkin in the bag.

Neil was waiting outside. "Just follow me."

Ben thought the disguise a feeble one, but nobody bothered him as he walked from the building. Perhaps they'd heard Mr Micklegate's strictures.

"Prêt again? We haven't much time," Neil suggested.

"Okay." Ben had seen enough of the lawyer to know that if they went to a more upmarket restaurant, Neil would add the cost to his already exorbitant bill. Anyway, the easiest place to vanish in London was in a crowd. Still in the bright waistcoat, Ben tagged along as Neil cut a path through the swarming office workers enjoying the sunshine.

The aircon felt pleasantly decadent when they entered the bustling café. Neil nudged him. "You get a seat. Lunch is on me. What do you want?"

Adrenaline and apprehension had removed his appetite. Nevertheless, Ben asked for a cheese and pickle sandwich, crisps and an Americano coffee. He would force himself to eat. There was nowhere to sit, until he spotted a couple leaving a tiny table in the corner. It was heaped with empty cups and sandwich wrappers. Ben didn't move them, thinking they would act as a barrier to strangers.

"Is that chair free?"

Ben looked up. Amy slid into the empty place opposite him.

When he emerged from the queue, Neil would have to look elsewhere. There was no way Ben was missing this opportunity. "Help yourself. How did you find me?"

Amy laughed, dimpling her cheeks attractively. "Serendipity. I wasn't looking."

"Weren't you with Dee Saxton?"

"Dad wanted to take her somewhere nice to cheer her up. I didn't hang about to rain on their parade."

Kat fronted Starshine vodka, but Amy, who worked behind the scenes, was prettier. Ben took his iPhone from a pocket. "I always meant to ask for your number."

"I've got a boyfriend."

Why had she sought him out, then? "That's no kind of answer. Either you'll give me your number or you won't: yes or no?"

She reeled off the digits, and he tapped them into his phone. A tinkling sound emerged from her flowery backpack when he rang.

"What do you think the verdict's going to be?" Amy chewed her lip.

"I don't know." He paused, wondering why she'd asked.

"You must be worried. It could affect your future."

"Yes. I am, and it does." Why should he lie to her? "The police said they'd take no further action. They might reconsider if the jury decides it was unlawful killing."

"I know you're not a murderer." Amy's blue eyes were wide with sympathy. "Dee told me everything."

"She told the police, too. They listened. I just hope the jury did."

Chapter 3.   Kat

"Are we reviewing sales figures or having a snooze?" Marty Bridges demanded.

Kat snapped back to attention. "Sorry." She returned her glance from the window to the huge screen on Marty's wall, wishing she was outside and running far away from this office in Birmingham. Since she fled from the courtroom, she'd had a single awkward conversation with Tim. Now they were both in the same Monday morning meeting, he was hard to avoid. At least he couldn't ask questions that weren't about vodka.

"Just take a look at that graph. Starshine vodka: the best investment I ever made." Marty chortled, lounging back in his padded leather office chair, hands clasped behind his bald head. It glistened under the spotlights set into the ceiling above.

"Told you, Dad." Tim was copying Marty's body language, or at any rate, as much as the S-shaped meeting chair would allow. He couldn't park his feet on the table in front of him as Marty had on his desk.

Kat had dim memories of Marty twenty-five years before, when he'd bought vodka from her late father's plant in Bazakistan. Riding a motorbike and carrying a case full of dollars, swashbuckling Marty had arrived just as the country emerged from the yoke of the Soviet Union. Then, her business partner had been slim and handsome like Tim, not fat and balding. It was scary to think that Tim's wavy fair hair would vanish and his waistline expand to resemble Marty's one day.

She recognised that their personalities were different, though. Tim was easy-going, while Marty was controlling: too much so. He'd contributed all the capital in their joint venture, using that leverage to pull the strings.

Panelled in bird's eye maple with a plush cream carpet, this room had been designed for Marty's comfort and self-importance. Its opulence belied the rest of the office suite. A single storey tacked onto his central Birmingham warehouse, it was as functional as the pipes in her distillery.

She glared past Amy at the father and son, irritation surpassing the unease she felt around Tim. "My vodka didn't make itself."

"Or market itself," Amy said.

Marty scowled, then seemed to think better of it. "All right, credit where it's due," he admitted. "You've done a tremendous job ramping up production, Kat, and Amy's marketing strategy was spot on. The new distillery paid for itself in less than half a year." He beamed.

"We could easily increase production too," Kat said. "We'd have to buy more pipes and vats, but there's plenty of room. That building is huge." It was a modern brick box, acquired by Marty at auction, and in reasonable condition. That made it different from most of his other properties, those ramshackle former factories close to Birmingham city centre. They were prime candidates for gentrification, but that would never happen to the new distillery. It was just off a ring road, in a zone that was solidly industrial. Kat didn't care for the area much. There were no charming coffee bars where she could meet Tim. Perhaps that was just as well.

"Can't you squeeze more out of the equipment you've got?" Marty asked. "There's been a spike in orders even in the last few days."

Tim glanced at Kat, his blue eyes wide with a blend of emotions: concern, curiosity and wariness fighting each other.

Kat looked away. "You might as well say it. It's the effect of all the publicity for the inquest. Amy predicted that."

"No verdict as yet, I see. Your picture will be on the front page of the red tops when it's announced. Imagine what that will do for revenues," Marty said.

There was a long silence. Kat forced herself to study the graph, mentally translating its curves into production flows.

Tim made an obvious effort to change the subject. "You'll see we're expecting an uptick in sales in the second half of the year, as we approach Christmas. The November ad campaign's already planned."

"Make it a Starshine Christmas," Amy added.

"That's your strapline?" Marty asked.

"Yes," Amy said. "We're backing it up with a limited edition sequinned bottle sleeve. It both looks good and keeps the vodka cool."

"The beauty is that we can use the same idea on other seasonal occasions, like Valentine's Day," Tim said. "All we have to do is change the design. I think they'll become collectors' items."

"Make sure you keep a few back for me," Marty said.

Kat lost patience. "Marty, the answer to your question from five minutes ago is yes, I can make enough to meet Tim's sales forecasts without buying new kit. There's only 10% headroom, though. And to answer the question you didn't ask, I have just enough time to distil vodka as well as taking part in all the PR opportunities Amy has organised for me."

"Our consumers love you, Kat," Amy said.

"Well, they're all young people too, enjoying a party lifestyle," Marty said. "Am I right, or am I right?"

"If only we went to parties," Amy said.

Kat knew what she meant. Before coming to Birmingham, the two girls had shared a flat in London. Always short of money, they'd still had an enviable social life. Youth and beauty opened doors to exclusive events. Now, settled into relationships and busy jobs, they rarely enjoyed the vodka they worked so hard to make and sell. The sparkle seemed to have vanished from their lives.

Tim appeared to tune into her thoughts. "I'll take you out on the town tonight, Kat," he offered. "There's a new cocktail bar you'll love. I've just persuaded them to take Starshine."

"I'm busy," she said.

"Let's get a coffee together after the meeting, then."

"Sorry, I'm having one with Amy. We've got business to discuss."

Amy managed not to betray the surprise she undoubtedly felt. There were no snarky comments from Marty, either, as he drew the meeting to a close.

"Coffee at Tom's Kitchen?" Kat asked Amy. On the way to the railway station, it was a casual dining space in the Mailbox, a glitzy development of shops and bars.

Amy's eyes shone. "You're on."

Kat hurried Amy out of the building. Her phone buzzed as they crossed the busy main road that bisected their route. It had to be Tim. Kat ignored it.

"So what are we meeting about?" Amy asked.

"Just shooting the breeze."

"Marty will want to know."

"Don't let him dominate you," Kat said. "You're his marketing manager. That implies responsibility and trust."

Amy frowned. They'd arrived at the coffee bar. She went to the counter to order drinks, while Kat sank into a velvet banquette, calmed by smooth jazz in the background.

Light streamed through large windows, catching the leaves of tall spiky plants in pots. Kat yawned. She hadn't slept well since her day in court. Caffeine would be most welcome.

"Black coffee for you, Kat," Amy said, handing over a takeaway cup. Her own would contain a skinny latte. "What's with you and Tim?"

"We're going through a rocky patch."

"Why? You're supposed to be getting married. I thought you were moving in together. What's the problem?"

Before she replied, Kat looked around, unwilling to be overheard. "Our sex life isn't great."

"Mine could be better, too," Amy admitted.

Kat sighed. "I don't enjoy making love. Not since the miscarriage. I'm so afraid of falling pregnant."

"Aren't you taking precautions?"

"I'm on the pill, so it shouldn't be a problem, but suppose I forget to take one? That's how I ended up expecting before. I don't think I'm fit to be a mother, when I couldn't even protect my child before it was born." Kat rubbed moisture from her eyes.

"That wasn't your fault. It was Shaun Halloran's, and he's dead. It's not going to happen again." Amy bit her lip. "Isn't Tim sympathetic?"

"He's been patient with me for over a year, but the inquest is chewing him up. Now, he suspects I lost the baby because Shaun Halloran tried…" She didn't want to say more. "Actually, Shaun thumped me, hard, and I think that's why I had the miscarriage. I'd already told Tim that Shaun didn't do anything… intimate."

"He may have wanted to."

"Probably," Kat had no doubts. "But he didn't get the chance. His son rescued us."

"Ben Halloran is a good guy. Nothing like his father," Amy said.

"I wouldn't go that far, my dear. He must have impressed you at the inquest."

Amy suddenly blushed. "We met him before, remember?"

"I remember too well." Kat trembled. There was something about his eyes – the spitting image of his father's. She said, fiercely, "You shouldn't have let him chat you up in that bar. You're going out with my brother."

"Erik's always working. 'Going out' is something we just don't seem to do anymore." Amy drew blood from her lip this time. "Anyway, it was just a conversation with Ben. Nothing says I can't talk to him. Shouldn't you sort out your own love life before you interfere in mine?"

"Well, what do you think I should do?"

"What you should have done already. Go out with Tim and get hammered. You've been driving yourself too hard."

Kat nodded. Keeping busy had stopped her thinking about the miscarriage, her grief and her guilt. Her baby wouldn't have died if she hadn't attracted Shaun into her life. Sensing more tears beginning to form, she let them roll down her cheek. Crying brought comfort.

Amy hugged her. "You and Tim will pull through, Kat. After a few drinks, you'll kiss and make up. He wanted to see you tonight, didn't he? It's not too late to say you made a mistake and you're free after all. Blame me. Tell him you thought we had a girls' night planned, but actually I'm off to London."

"Are you really? Why?"

"Marketing meetings."

"In the evening?"

"In the afternoon, but I'm staying over at my dad's place. Anyway, why the third degree?"

Kat fell silent, her mind a maelstrom of doubts. A needling voice whispered to her that Amy was seeing Ben Halloran. Was Amy bored with Erik? Why would Ben meet her: was he really attracted to the thin redhead, or would he use Amy to get closer to Kat and avenge his father? Fear teased Kat's spine. Desperately, she told herself the notion was fantastical.

Amy sipped her foamy latte, a prickly expression on her features as she waited for an answer.

Chapter 4.　　Ben

Two messages flashed up on his computer screen simultaneously: one from Neil Curtis and the other from Amy. Ben opened the lawyer's first.

'Good news. Please ring. Neil,' he read.

Ben called him.

"The jury's delivered its verdict. Death by misadventure." Neil's smile was palpable in his voice.

Ben caught an odd sound of gurgling water in the background, He hardly noticed as relief surged through him. It wasn't unlawful killing. He punched the air.

"I expect you're pleased?" Neil didn't wait for a response. "Now you can really move on. I thought it was the way it would go, but you can never be sure. Where were you earlier, by the way? I've been ringing you constantly since they gave Micklegate their report. I had to duck into the gents to escape the press."

"I was wearing headphones." He'd been anxious about the verdict from the minute he awoke, and all weekend before that. Only a video game with a loud rock soundtrack could distract him from his fears. He managed to add, "Thanks."

"You're welcome. You can talk to the media all you want, now, but I wouldn't advise it. I've prepared a short statement I can read out to them on your behalf, if you like. Want me to email it to you?"

Ben said that he would. It arrived within thirty seconds of the phone call's end, proving that Neil had written it in advance. The lawyer had doubtless penned alternatives for each possible verdict.

This version, in surprisingly clear English, expressed sorrow for the injuries suffered by Kat and Dee, and thanked them and the jury. Ben did not condone Shaun's criminal lifestyle but regretted inadvertently causing his father's death. He had now lost both his parents, his mother having died of cancer seven years before. Ben loved them both and would always miss them.

Ben sent a single word reply: 'Fine'. The emotions he really felt towards Shaun Halloran were too complicated to express in a couple of paragraphs. Neil's banal announcement should satisfy the press.

It occurred to him that Jon wouldn't be happy. Jon was safely behind bars, however, at least for now. Ben forgot all about his brother once he read Amy's message. 'In London tonight. Want to meet as friends?'

31

Ben grinned. Why not? He had plenty to celebrate. Once she knew him better, he'd persuade her to take friendship to another level.

Chapter 5.   Marty

Looking through the window, Marty Bridges saw the sky darken. He picked up an umbrella, a long, harlequin-coloured number with the name of his bank emblazoned on it. It had been acquired on a golf day. Since then, his wife had refused to have it on display in their freshly decorated house. He hoped she wouldn't think it too loud for the tasteful environs of the Malmaison, where she'd agreed to meet him for lunch.

A few spots of rain splashed onto the bright canopy as he strolled outside into Florence Street. It was a strip of ancient brick factory buildings, most now put to other uses and some in the process of demolition. The gentrification begun by the Mailbox complex was extending here. Marty walked past newish hotels, flats and shops.

Halfway to his destination, he bumped into Amy, scurrying back to work with her jacket held above her head to fend off the burgeoning shower.

"Thought you were going to London?" Marty asked.

"I've got to collect my laptop and files."

Marty tutted. The Mailbox was near the station. If she were better organised, she'd have taken them with her earlier.

The Malmaison hotel and brasserie was at the furthest end of the old sorting office development. Angela favoured it because there was a spa, where she liked to meet her friends for pampering and prosecco. Setting eyes on her, Marty realised she'd indulged this morning. Her face, always artfully creamed and coloured, had the glow of a cosmetician's treatment.

She was perching daintily in one of the brasserie's booths, a slim, elfin woman who seemed nothing like her fifty-one years. If there was any grey in his second wife's short, curly blonde locks, her hairdresser wouldn't let Marty find it. She wore an indigo lace blouse and skinny blue jeans, both of which brought out the colour of her eyes.

"I've ordered prosecco," she told him. "What are you having, Marty?"

"Guinness, please." A waiter had appeared without being summoned.

They asked for food: a chargrilled steak and chips for him, a salad for her.

Drinks arrived. "Cheers," Angela said, clinking glasses and taking a sip of fizz. "Isn't this lovely – chilling out?"

"Cheers." Marty swigged his pint. "I can manage a couple of these – after all, I have something to celebrate. I've got planning permission for student flats in Florence Street."

Angela gasped. "That's wonderful. Now you can sell up and move your warehouse, wouldn't it be a good opportunity to wind down yourself? Your kids are perfectly capable of running the firm."

"Not the way I do."

"What's wrong with new ideas? I bet Tim has plenty, and Kat can help him."

Marty bristled. "Four children, four equal shares." He wasn't giving everything to his eldest son, especially as he suspected Kat would be in charge when she married Tim.

Angela seemed pleased. "It sounds like you've been thinking about it."

"I have, but it's complicated. Don't forget, two of my companies are joint ventures. One of those is Darria Enterprises, and it's losing money. None of the kids have the experience to turn it around. I'm struggling to manage it myself."

"Why not sell the company, then?"

Marty had to admit that it was a shrewd suggestion. He could seek a buyer for his 50% shareholding, anyway. While he'd fall out with his friend and business partner, Erik White, perhaps that was a price worth paying. He'd get time and money back.

His lack of response was treated as a sign of agreement. "You could work part-time for a few months, then retire altogether. I've been looking at cruises." Angela reached into her capacious handbag, which was easily the size of a man's briefcase and out of all proportion to her petite frame.

"What's hiding in the black hole today?" Marty asked. He could guess.

Proudly, Angela displayed a generous sheaf of glossy brochures in a fan shape around his beer glass.

"So many boats, so little time," Marty said, overwhelmed by the choices and underwhelmed at the prospect. His business had overcome many challenges, and in his heart, he knew it would survive his departure. He had no objection to retiring and enjoying himself, but his preferred mode of sightseeing was a long distance road trip, wind whistling through what remained of his hair.

If Angela detected his lack of enthusiasm for cruises, she ignored it. She was clearly enthralled by these floating hotels with spa treatments on tap, unlimited prosecco and the requirement to buy a whole new wardrobe before sailing. She pointed a finger, tipped with a perfect coral oval, at the largest and shiniest booklet.

"Joanne did this one after she split with Bob. Four weeks in the Caribbean. She came back with a tan and a new partner."

"Are you threatening me?" Marty teased her.

Angela winked. "It won't happen if we go together."

Marty sighed. No way was Angela going to learn to ride a motorbike or even agree to drive across Europe in his Jaguar convertible. "Choose the one you like best, bab."

Angela's eyes sparkled. "Really? I've been asking you for so long, I thought you'd never say yes."

"I'm not making promises yet. I need to talk to the kids." He'd discuss succession planning with Kat and Erik, his joint venture partners, too. There were bound to be arguments with the ambitious Kat, but Marty was ready for them. He wouldn't let her push his children out of the business empire he'd worked so hard to build.

Chapter 6.   Erik

Costs were spiralling upwards. Erik White wasn't a financial whizz kid, but as a scientist, he had no trouble with mathematics. Invoices for the forthcoming clinical trials were several hundred thousand pounds higher than he'd expected.

Developing a cancer cure was never going to be cheap; he acknowledged that. Perhaps he should have done a deal with a deep-pocketed pharmaceutical company. That would have meant abandoning hope of a drug accessible to all, though. With a few exceptions, medicines produced by Big Pharma were affordable only to patients in rich countries.

It had seemed like the solution to all his problems when Marty Bridges, his old friend and mentor, had offered to fund the research in exchange for a 50% stake. They'd agreed on milestones and budgets. Four years later, the business was still underperforming. While Marty had seemed philosophical when the herbal tea they sold as a sideline failed to do well, Erik sensed his joint venture partner had lost patience by now.

Shoulders hunched, Erik tapped at his laptop, opening the contracts he'd signed for the work. Comparing them with the bills in front of him, he saw he was being asked to pay for services outside the scope of the agreements. All the extras were desirable, however; they'd been discussed in emails, and he'd approved them. He just hadn't appreciated they were so pricy. Wrapped up in research, working long hours and suffering pointed remarks from Amy because of it, he hadn't updated the budgets properly. Marty would be furious.

Erik got up, stretched, and went to make tea in the kitchenette. He didn't keep a samovar boiling as his mother had done when he was a child, but he at least adhered to the Russian tradition by using leaves and a pot. Adding three spoons of honey to his mug, he returned to his desk.

The office in Birmingham's Jewellery Quarter, shared with several freelance staff and owned by Marty like the attic flat Erik rented above it, was empty except for him. This was the usual state of affairs after five o'clock. Erik's self-employed co-workers, if they behaved like ships at all, were the kind he passed during the day.

Restlessly, he paced across the room, stopping occasionally to sip tea. He was concerned more for Marty's disappointment than his wrath. His friend had hoped for quicker returns. Amy had heard Marty was deferring retirement because Darria Enterprises' finances were so bad.

Amy was someone else Erik had managed to annoy without effort. His girlfriend would be attending her grandparents' golden wedding solo this weekend, as Erik had too much work to travel to Chislehurst for the party. He wondered how he could make amends.

The strains of Prokofiev's 'Dance of the Knights' jolted him from his soul-searching. His phone, set to vibrate as well as ring, was bouncing on his desk. The caller had masked their number, but Erik swiped upwards anyway.

"Hello, it's Erik."

"Why so low, my lad?" There was no mistaking the sweet, throaty voice, especially as the phrase was delivered in Russian.

"Mother. To what do I owe the pleasure?"

"Oh, you know. I like to talk."

He could virtually hear her shrug. It was true that, since that day two years ago when he'd discovered that she was miraculously still alive, she'd phoned him once a month. There was never much to say, not least because Erik refused to gossip. His mother had given up asking after Marty, whom she hated, and Kat, who loathed her. Erik didn't share his sister's revulsion, but he respected her privacy. He didn't trust their mother either.

"How's the weather in Bazakistan?" he asked.

She giggled. "That's a very English remark."

"I am English now." With Marty's help, both he and Kat had anglicised their surnames when they claimed political asylum more than a decade before. Then, as far as they knew, their parents were dead. It would never have occurred to Erik that his mother, a secret agent, had signed his father's death warrant.

"How is the darria herb growing in England?" she asked.

"Fine. It's like a weed in Bazakistan, and it's suited to conditions in the fields outside Birmingham too." That information was already in the public domain.

"And your research? You've extracted the active ingredient?"

"I did that years ago. We're just doing another round of trials, now." He added sharply, as an ominous thought occurred to him, "You're not ill, are you? You know you can drink darria as an infusion, like tea, if you are? I thought you already did, actually." It was reputed to have anti-ageing properties.

She laughed, clearly amused. "Silly boy! No, I'm not sick, and yes, I drink the tea every morning. My skin is so smooth."

"Marty's wife likes it too." Again, he wasn't betraying a confidence; Angela had given magazine interviews to hype the darria teabags that Erik and Marty were selling.

"The darria herb could be Bazakistan's most promising export, after oil and vodka. That brings me to a business proposition I'd like to discuss." Her tone was suddenly brisk and professional.

"Thanks, but I'm busy enough; I can't start anything new." He didn't want commercial ties. Marty had already burned his fingers buying poisoned vodka from her.

"It's not a new venture. It's the boost you need to make your dream work. You avoided selling out to the big pharmaceutical companies, so your drug would be inexpensive" – he hadn't told her this, but it, too, had featured in the media – "so you're short of money to invest. I know you must be, because you're relying on Marty Bridges for funds, and he drives a hard bargain."

She wasn't wrong. Erik remained silent, curious despite the alarm bells ringing throughout his brain.

"Darria comes from Bazakistan. It's a well-known fact. Your cancer cure should be made in Bazakistan too. The President wants you to bring it back home. Five million dollars of public money will be made available immediately to invest in clinical trials. You'll receive a salary of two hundred thousand dollars a year, a house and a car."

"A presidential vanity project?"

"More than that. Showing the world that Bazaki skills can make a real difference. We're not just a nation of oil wells and drunk horse traders." She paused, a note of triumph in her voice. "So, what do you say?"

"Marty is my partner in Darria Enterprises, as you know. He'd never agree."

"Marty will do anything if the money's right."

Would he? Erik hoped she was wrong. However strong the lure of cash, or the love he still felt for his mother, they wouldn't persuade him to return to Bazakistan. Nor would patriotism: any loyalty owed to his homeland had died with his father.

Running a successful export business hadn't saved Sasha Belov from the firing squad. Why should his son risk the same fate?

Chapter 7.   Kat

The tram's doors slid open. A handful of commuters exited onto the platform. Kat had rarely seen many others use the Jewellery Quarter station, possibly because it was such a short walk from Birmingham city centre. She was in a hurry, however. Having caught a rush hour train near the distillery, she'd suffered an unscheduled halt, staring at disused factories on the approach to New Street. There, she'd hopped on the bright pink tram. To her dismay, it seemed to creep like a snail.

The tram stop elicited a sensation of being at the bottom of a gorge, as the line ran along a cutting. Kat had to scale several flights of stairs to ground level. At last, she dashed past the ticket office, the hopeful beggars sitting on the pavement, and the jewellers' glittering windows. Her destination was the Rose Villa Tavern, an ornate red brick pub built a century before to serve the area's gold and silversmiths.

Within, sunlight shone through arched stained-glass windows, dousing the bar's patrons with speckles of colour. She scanned the large, busy room. Over six feet tall, Tim was usually easy to spot. Frowning, Kat checked her phone. He'd messaged to say he was running late too.

There were no seats in the bar. She headed for a snug off to the side, rather hoping it would be empty on this late spring evening. It was a cosy, windowless area with leather armchairs, popular in the winter, when a fire was lit.

"We must stop meeting like this." A twenty pound note in hand, Marty Bridges waited while beer was poured for him.

"I'll have a Cosmopolitan, please."

"I'd expect nothing else." Marty's chuckle didn't reach his eyes. He turned to the barmaid. "Make her cocktail with Starshine, please."

"Kat, over here." Her brother, Erik, was sitting in an armchair next to the bare fireplace.

A decade older than Kat, Erik gave the impression of even greater maturity. It seemed to her that she was looking at her late father's twin: tall and thin, spiky black hair cropped close to his scalp. It wasn't just his appearance that Erik shared with Alexander Belov, the man his family and friends called Sasha. Her brother had inherited kindness, idealism and a serious manner.

As Erik gestured, patting the seat opposite, Kat pictured herself as a child, following her father around the distillery as he expounded on his secret tips for vodka manufacture. She blinked a tear from her eye. It didn't matter if her brother saw it, but she wouldn't show weakness in front of Marty.

The businessman fetched their drinks from the bar and pulled over another chair.

"Aren't you guys having a meeting?" Kat asked.

"It's finished," Marty said. "We're on the social chit-chat now."

Erik raised his pint glass. "Cheers, Marty. What brings you in from the sunshine, Kat?"

"I'm seeing Tim. He should be here by now."

"Stuck in traffic," Marty said. "He reckons the gridlock at junction 8 of the M6 is worse than usual. The Highways Agency should employ a parking attendant to issue tickets." He yawned and stretched, knocking back half of his pint. "I won't stay long. Angela wants me home to look at cruise brochures."

"Has she finally pinned you down?" Erik sounded sceptical.

Marty chortled. "Nothing's booked yet." He finished his drink, smacking his lips. "An excellent drop of beer. Too bad that I must love you and leave you."

"What was your meeting about?" Kat asked, as soon as Marty was gone.

"Next steps for my cancer research." Erik's green eyes betrayed concern. "It's turned out more expensive than Marty hoped."

"He knew the risks when he agreed to invest."

"Maybe, but he regrets the investment now. Costs are higher than we both expected, and it's bothering him. There's a stage payment due next week. He said if it hadn't been for strong sales of Starshine, he couldn't afford it."

Kat made a mental note to ask Marty for access to Starshine vodka's accounts. Other than drawing a salary every month, thankfully a much larger one than when she started, she hadn't paid much attention to its cash flows. Had she been sleepwalking on Monday? Marty had actually said her new distillery had paid for itself within six months. His old Snow Mountain vodka brand belonged to him, but Starshine was a joint venture. She was entitled to half of its profits, and it was about time they found their way to her.

"What's wrong, Kat?"

She forced herself to pull her focus away from money, and the difference that income from Starshine might make when she and Tim finally bought a house together. "Sorry. Miles away."

"It's an odd coincidence you should say that. I heard from our mother yesterday. She rang from Bazakistan."

A pang of loss caught Kat unawares. Whether the emotion was triggered by the mention of her treacherous parent or equally perfidious homeland, she wasn't sure. Shakily, she put her drink down. "Why did she call?"

"She had a business proposal," Erik said.

"I hope you told her where to go. What was it?"

"I politely declined," Erik said. "She'd suggested before she could secure a research post for me at Kireniat University. Now, she's upped the ante. The President wants a cancer cure 'made in Bazakistan'. She told me he'd personally authorised her to offer funding of five million dollars and a salary of two hundred thousand dollars a year."

Kat's mouth gaped. "They're really trying hard. That's like winning the lottery."

"Until the moment there's a bullet in your head. I had to refuse. I don't trust our mother, the President, or the state of Bazakistan. They all played a part in our father's death."

"She didn't try to claim Father was a political agitator again?"

Erik held up his hands. "Who knows if it was true? One thing's for sure, the country desperately needed export earnings when the Soviet Union fell apart, and Father's sales of vodka to Marty Bridges delivered that precious foreign currency. It wasn't enough to save his life when the President decided, for whatever reason, that it was forfeit. That tells me even if I produce a world-class cancer treatment, I could disappear in an instant at the President's whim."

"Did you talk to Marty? He owns half the rights to the darria drug, I suppose. I mean, you're partners in this." Kat pursed her lips. Erik's research sounded more valuable than she'd appreciated. As usual, Marty was profiting from someone else's efforts.

"We discussed it, among other things." Erik seemed keen to change the subject. "I'm relieved to hear you're seeing Tim. Is everything fine between you two again?"

Kat shook her head. "Not really, but it won't get better unless we talk."

"I hope you work things out. Tim's a decent sort."

"I think so too. He's a keeper." Kat pulled a face. "I can't understand why our relationship suddenly got complicated. How about you and Amy?"

A flicker of alarm registered on his serious features. "What's she been saying?"

"Not much. You don't spend enough time together." Kat wondered if that was all. She was convinced Amy had secrets.

"It's odd. She's said nothing to me, Kat, but somehow I feel her slipping away from me. I can't work it out."

"You could try taking her out..."

Before she'd finished speaking, Kat felt a hand on her shoulder. She knew that aftershave.

Turning, she saw Tim smile in a way that made her quiver.

"Hi, Erik. How goes it with you? Not interrupting anything, am I?"

Erik stood, stretching. "Of course not. No worries, I'll leave you guys in peace."

"You can stay if you like," Kat whispered, torn between the urge to help him and her longing for Tim.

"No, got to go."

"Catch you later," Tim said to Erik's back as he hurried away. He picked up Kat's empty cocktail glass. "You started without me, I see. Another Cosmopolitan?"

The barmaid was ready. "With Starshine again?" she asked.

"Of course." Tim turned to wink at Kat. "That's impressive. You're doing my job for me, Kat."

"It's your dad you have to thank."

"Was he in earlier? I forgot this was his second home." Tim put the drinks on a low table, and pulled a chair close to hers before sitting down. He looked into her eyes. "I'm sorry, Kat, I've been an idiot."

Was he saying he believed her? "You know, nothing happened – except what I told the coroner's court. It was hard even talking about that. I just wanted to forget about the baby, and about ever being pregnant. It was the only way I could cope."

Tim took her hand, and squeezed it gently. "I let my imagination trick me," he said. "I couldn't bear to think of that man touching you."

Kat closed her eyes. That was a mistake; memories clawed at her mind like hungry ghosts. Her shoulders tensed. "He just hit me," she said. "It was enough."

"I know." Tim enveloped her in his arms. "I was crazy to think otherwise."

"Why should it make a difference?" she challenged. "I'm not a child; I've had boyfriends."

He frowned. "I wasn't rational. Hearing your evidence was a shock. I knew it had been a brutal attack, but I hadn't appreciated the nuances. I thought you'd been holding something back from me. Forgive me."

Kat nestled into him, familiar sensations of attraction flowing through her as she raised her lips to his.

Tim kissed her. "Friends again?"

"More than that, don't you think?"

"Come back home with me."

"You bet." Standing up, she pulled him to his feet.

As they walked arm in arm to his car, Kat could feel her heartbeat dancing with the raindrops on the pavement.

Once he'd parked the gold Subaru, Tim took her hand. The thrill tugged her closer to him, as if she were melting into him. They kissed, remaining entwined as they shuffled into the boxy apartment block's lobby and up to the first floor. Stumbling inside the flat, they headed for the sofa, kicking the door closed behind them.

Bathed in light from the huge window, Tim's hair shone like a golden halo. "Alone at last."

Kat didn't let him say more. She kissed him, taking the tip of her tongue to his.

Tim stroked her hair, tracing a finger down her spine and squeezing her buttocks. "Let me undress you."

She lay back on the furry cushions, her body tingling with anticipation.

Tim took his time, caressing and kissing her skin as he removed her silver sandals, her top, and her skinny jeans. Finally, he started on the pink wisps of her silk and lace underwear.

"I gave you these." He sounded surprised and delighted to see them.

"Yes, and they're beautiful." Kat had chosen them that morning, packing contraceptive pills in her handbag, too. She wouldn't get pregnant, she told herself, allowing her senses to surrender to his touch. A wave of desire pulsed through her.

Tim eased the delicate scraps of cloth from her body. "They're pretty things, but it's you who are beautiful."

While he peeled her clothing away with reverence, his garments were swiftly removed and thrown randomly on the floor. He knelt before her, kissing her thighs, bringing his tongue between them.

Kat gasped as he found a sweet spot. His hands reached to squeeze her nipples, and she was unable to stop moaning his name as pleasure suffused her entire body.

When he stopped, she pulled him upwards and towards her, guiding him inside. Beginning gently, his lovemaking quickened and deepened as she wriggled against him. They both cried out when they reached a peak together, sunset's colours playing over them.

Later, once they had crawled between the sheets of Tim's pristine bed, Kat watched him sleep. She pressed her lips to his forehead, pale in the ghostly sheen of moonbeams slinking through the curtain's edge. Tiptoeing out of the bedroom, she switched on the light in the lounge, found her handbag and retrieved a pill. She headed to the kitchen for a glass of water.

The cold liquid and bright lights cut into her trance. She wanted to be with Tim forever, but not here. However cosy, the flat was too small for them. They could afford somewhere larger if she received her profits from Starshine. She mustn't forget it was time for Marty to pay his dues.

Chapter 8.   Marty

Paying suppliers was one of Marty Bridge's least favourite tasks, on a par with sitting in the dentist's chair. It wasn't so much the stream of money flowing from his bank account that annoyed him, but the boring, repetitive processes. Although his bookkeeper prepared payments for him to authorise, he still had to remember different passwords for multiple screens, click buttons and check numbers. Perhaps the bad old days hadn't been so dire. Without online banking, he'd have to sign sixty cheques at a stretch; was it really worse than this?

A phone call was a pleasant distraction, despite the twinge of trepidation when Marty recognised the number. "Hello, Kat. No trouble, I hope?"

"I wanted to speak privately." Kat's tone was crisp. "When we had our planning meeting, you said sales of Starshine were going well. I'll run close to capacity to fulfil Starshine and Snow Mountain orders for Christmas."

"Yes, it's all good news."

"Right. We were discussing sales and production volumes, but we didn't look at cash and profits. I want to see the financials."

That was typical of Kat: at the first sign that the business was flush with funds, she was angling for a pay rise. "You can trust me to take care of those," Marty said. "You make sure the bottles come out of the distillery, and I'll do the rest. I've been running East West Bridges longer than you've been on this earth."

"Yes, and it would have gone under last year without my help," Kat said, reminding him of an unwelcome fact. "I'm a 50% shareholder in Starshine vodka, Marty, and I'm entitled to more management information than I'm getting. If the company's making as much money as you hinted, it's time it paid a dividend."

"You're taking a salary," Marty pointed out, reasonably, he thought.

"It's not enough."

That was the crux of the matter. Marty was sure Kat harboured a shopping addiction. Angela frequently complimented her on a new dress or make-up, and both women discussed boutiques far too knowledgeably for his liking. He should be thankful, he supposed, that Kat wanted to earn cash for her extravagance herself rather than sponge off his son.

"Hello. Are you still there?" Kat asked.

Marty nodded at the phone, adding, "It's not appropriate to pay a dividend, Kat. It's true that cash flows from Starshine have been strong. It's enabled me to repay the loans I borrowed" – he corrected himself – "that we borrowed, to buy the distillery building and all the equipment in it. Oh, and fund Amy's highly successful viral marketing campaign. There's no dosh to spare right now. Sorry."

"Maybe we need to run Starshine differently from your other ventures," Kat said. "Send me the profit and loss account, Marty, please. Then we should have a meeting next week once I've been through it."

Still outraged at her cheek, Marty sent an email to Annika, his niece and part-time bookkeeper. She was away for a few days with her children, but on her return, she could produce figures to satisfy Kat. He much preferred to keep a close eye on the bank account. Cash was all that mattered; other numbers were smoke and mirrors.

Where had Kat learned to read a balance sheet anyway? Was it on the curriculum of the distilling courses she'd taken? When he'd left school at sixteen to make a living from buying anything he could sell, his only qualification had been his desire to escape the poverty in which he'd been raised. Marty had measured his success by money then, as now.

His PA, Tanya, popped her colourful head around his office door. Her bobbed hair, which he suspected was naturally grey like his remaining strands, was fairy cake pink today.

"Marty, while you were on the phone, Professor Blacklock called for you."

"Never heard of him."

"He's involved in the clinical trials for darria, and he's chasing the stage payment."

"I'll send it now."

His time wasn't his own. Marty returned his awareness to the screen in front of him. The email from Professor Charles Blacklock, attaching an invoice for nearly five hundred thousand pounds, was one of a batch forwarded by Annika for this morning's payment run. The university had changed its bank account details again. The good news was that they were using an old account already on his system, so the authorisation procedure was straightforward.

He made the transfer, along with others Annika had requested. Without even thinking of checking the hour on screen, he glanced at his Rolex. It was 4.30pm already. In thirty minutes, he was due to speak at a networking event, hosted by a modish bar in the Jewellery Quarter. It was barely a mile away, but roads would be slow on the cusp of the rush hour. Not only that, his usual route was closed because of the extended demolition of the city's old library. Although many loathed it, Marty had been fond of the upturned concrete pyramid. He wished it had been left alone; the development's position within a major roundabout brought traffic to a standstill.

Tanya buzzed him to ask if he was leaving yet.

"I'm just thinking about it," Marty admitted.

"Would you like a cab? The gathering is in a bar, and you do like a beer or two."

Marty laughed. "I'll be a good boy."

He donned his suit jacket and made for the car park, an area of hardstanding next to the office. While it was gated and fenced off, and thus reasonably secure, he wasn't keen to leave his silver F-type Jaguar there overnight. Starting the car, he drove in a semi-circle around the city centre, a circuitous course thanks to the roundabout's closure.

The journey gave him time to practice his talk. While the networking group mainly comprised men and women of mature years, like himself, they'd invited a group of students to hear tips on starting up a business. Marty wasn't sure his message would be popular. He intended to tell them that a degree was the last thing they needed; what was important was a can-do attitude and the willingness to take risks.

In the event, the students were fascinated when he described how he'd travelled to Bazakistan with little more than a motorbike and a fistful of dollars.

"After the Berlin Wall came down and the Soviet Union imploded, the East was a mad place," he said. "There was excitement in the air. There were opportunities. There was also danger. I was an amateur boxer. Even so, I slept with a knife under my pillow, and I knew how to use it. You wouldn't need to do that today, but you had to then."

"You were kidnapped in Bazakistan only two years ago, and held as a hostage for ransom, weren't you?" one of the youths asked.

"You've googled me," Marty said, to knowing nods. "That's right. I was careless, and didn't check the credentials of the so-called estate agents who offered to drive me out of town to view a property. But a knife wouldn't have saved me from four men with a gun. So, the lesson to learn from that is: always check who you're dealing with, and that you can trust them."

He sipped his Black Country Porter, a dark, coffeeish beer with a creamy head. The bar kept its real ales well, albeit the price made him wince. He wouldn't hurry back here.

"Any questions before I move on?" he asked.

The young people were silent. They stared at him intently, like children listening to a story.

"You may know that my business partner, Kat White, was kidnapped too."

A few of the males leered. It was satisfying proof that they'd heard of Kat and seen her picture. Amy had insisted that Kat must be the face of Starshine vodka. She'd done her homework; it was the most successful marketing campaign Marty had ever seen.

"It was lucky there were two of us, because we could work together to escape. As it happens, I've known Kat and her brother since that first visit to Bazakistan. Their father was making amazing vodka, and he was desperate to sell it in the West. I helped him do that, to our mutual benefit. We had all kinds of problems: shortages of raw materials and haulage capacity, availability of shipping licences, bandits. The dollars opened doors. Incredibly, there were no heists when exports began." A sweetener to the police had seen to that; they'd escorted his consignments to Kireniat airport.

"That was Snow Mountain vodka," Marty finished. "It made me a millionaire. If I'm honest, doesn't that demonstrate why it's worth taking risks? You have to be able to bounce back from adversity, and be creative with it, though. Whether it's a kidnapping, bankruptcy or a supply problem, it's up to you to find a way out."

He gave them ten minutes more for further questions, during which several of the students offered to work for him. Marty wasn't surprised. His upscale vodka brands were a powerful lure. The undergraduates probably imagined futures as barflies and vodka tasters. They'd think twice if they understood the tedium of running a production line, badgering customers for money and making payments to suppliers.

Finally, he was able to swallow the rest of his pint and check for messages. Erik had left several while the phone was set to silent.

Marty called him back. "Is it urgent, or can it wait?" he asked.

"It's just a quick one," Erik said. "Would you mind paying the university tomorrow? They phoned today to pursue their invoice."

"You too?" Marty asked. "No worries, Erik; I did the bank transfer earlier. Professor Charles Blacklock was most insistent."

"Who's he?" Erik asked.

Marty felt a void opening in his stomach. He was seized by an intense desire to refill his glass and drain it in one.

Chapter 9.   Kat

"These are the latest management accounts for Starshine," Annika said. The huge screen on the wall of Marty's office revealed several columns of figures.

Kat glanced at Marty in his leather swivel chair. For once, he was sitting upright, elbows on his desk and fingers steepled under his chin. His expression was unreadable.

Annika was in her early thirties, fresh-faced, with the same wavy fair hair as the rest of the Bridges family. Her short crop, denims and no-nonsense manner betrayed a woman who had no time for herself. "You'll see there's cash of two hundred and forty two thousand pounds," she said. "Most of that is earmarked to pay VAT and duty."

"I thought there would be more," Kat said.

"I told you before, Kat." Marty sounded impatient. "We had a loan to buy the factory and kit it out. We've used money coming in to repay that."

"I don't remember being involved in the decision." Kat recalled Marty presenting the acquisition of the property with a loan as a fait accompli. She hadn't disagreed with it then, but there had been no discussion about clearing the debt afterwards.

"It was a no-brainer." The buzzword sounded odd coming from Marty's lips. "Why pay interest when you don't have to?"

She and Tim would be paying plenty of it when they were mortgaged to the hilt. Still, it wasn't worth arguing the point further. Marty had taken action, and it couldn't be undone. "Let's go through bank statements for the last three months to see how the cash flows look," Kat said. "It'll help us decide what dividends to take in future."

Marty looked mutinous.

Annika's features were strained. "That won't be possible, Kat. All three companies share the same bank account. I have to split transactions between East West Bridges, Starshine and Darria Enterprises when I'm doing the books."

Kat gaped at her. "I've never run a business before, but..."

"Exactly," Marty interrupted. "That's clear from the naïve questions you're asking. There's no reason for me to do all the paperwork the bank needs to open more accounts, then pay them three sets of charges for the privilege of leaving money with them."

"But you're talking about separate firms, differently owned," Kat said. "East West Bridges is yours, Marty. No one can dispute that. Starshine is partly mine, though, just as Darria Enterprises is your partnership with Erik. You shouldn't be mixing their funds together."

"With respect," Marty said, his tone hinting at a total lack of it, "I've been in this game a long time, and I know what I'm doing. This way, I minimise the risk of an overdraft."

"We're overdrawn at the moment," Annika said. "But the charges are lower than they would be if one company was in the red and the others in the black."

"Why should I subsidise East West Bridges?" Kat asked.

Annika coughed. "It's Darria Enterprises, actually. There was a cyber fraud. They took nearly half a million."

Marty flashed a sharp glance at his niece.

Kat jumped to her feet. "Why didn't you tell me before?" she demanded. She couldn't imagine how a massive scam like that had happened. Marty was so careful with money.

"It's none of your business," Marty snapped. "And sit down."

Kat remained standing. "What about Erik? You have no right to keep it secret from him."

Surely Erik would have said something to her if he'd known? He'd be devastated, especially if the loss blocked progress with his cancer research. Worse, it might tempt him to fall back into their mother's arms again. Kat shuddered.

"Erik is fully aware," Marty said. "We've agreed the next set of trials is going ahead, no matter what. You'll appreciate there's nothing to spare for dividends."

Kat understood the subtext. Marty was telling her that if she pushed him too hard, her brother would suffer.

"I've told the bank. They're working to resolve it – or at least, their central fraud unit claims to be trying to recover the funds. They're unbelievably slow."

Kat noticed dark circles under Marty's eyes. She took her seat again, trying to bring her temper under control. The cash was gone. Arguing with Marty wouldn't change anything.

"Wait," she said. "Amy's dad is a cyber security specialist. Why not see if he can help?"

"Charles? He does something in IT." Marty clearly didn't understand what that might be. He jabbed at his phone. "Hello, Amy, can you come through to my office, please?"

Amy shuffled into the room hesitantly, making eye contact only with Kat. She appeared no more relaxed, awake or confident than her boss and his niece. Her skin was pale and free of make-up, the only saving grace being that her green dress suited her coppery hair. Kat supposed Erik had shared the problem with her.

"Amy, sit down," Marty commanded, gesturing to a meeting chair. "I'll ask Tanya for coffees. Can you tell me more about the work your father does?"

"It includes cyber security, right?" Annika asked.

Amy was forced to meet their eyes. "Yes," she said. "He's always giving talks about it."

"I remember," Marty said. "I think. Listen, Amy, we have an issue with a rogue bank transfer."

"Really?" Amy said.

She must already know and be playing dumb.

"Yes, really. Unfortunately. I assume that, as your father and my friend, Charles would give us some advice."

Hope flickered in Amy's eyes. "Of course he would, Marty. Shall we Skype him now?"

"He'll be at work, won't he?"

"He'd always take a call from me." Amy pointed to the big screen. "Let's try it with video. Do you have his number? You should ring him first, to make sure he's not on a vape break."

Marty checked his iPhone and began tapping it. "Charles? Are you free to talk? What's your Skype handle?"

The monitor on the wall had switched to sleep mode by now. Marty cajoled it back to life, typing on his keyboard until Charles's head and shoulders filled the screen.

Dark-haired, handsome and urbane, Charles smiled at them. "Hello, Amy. My goodness, a cast of thousands. What's this about?"

"I've lost a substantial amount in an invoice fraud," Marty said.

"Let me guess," Charles said, "It was an existing supplier with a new bank account. Allegedly."

"Something like that," Marty muttered.

"There's a lot of it going on. Usually, what happens is that someone hacks into your IT system. That'll be when there's an open port."

"I beg your pardon?" Marty said.

Kat, for once, had some sympathy for him. She didn't know what Charles was talking about either.

"Think of a port as a portal, or door, into your network," Charles said. "You have to open it to allow information to flow in or out of the system through the web. For instance, you might use webmail, or hold your accounting data online. It allows your staff do their jobs when they're not in the office."

"One or two of the mums have flexible working," Marty said. "Annika often logs on at home or in a coffee bar, don't you, Annika?"

"Do you use public wi-fi?" Amy asked.

Annika looked sheepish.

Marty glowered at her.

"Let's not pre-judge anything, Marty. Somewhere, and there could be any number of ways to do it, a hacker has found a port that's open. What commonly happens next is that they guess a system administrator's password. That's easier than you might think. They'd use a computer programme to make thousands of guesses at the password, until it gets lucky. Sometimes, it doesn't take much. You wouldn't believe the number of people who use '123456' or 'password'. Just google it. The cracker software will try the most popular combinations first."

"I'm not completely ignorant. We always use strong passwords," Marty said.

"It doesn't matter. The cracker will get it right eventually. Then you're wide open to mischief, like emails with fake invoices."

"What I don't understand," Marty said, "is that the bank account where I sent the money was already on our system."

"An administrator would usually have the power to change supplier bank account details in your purchase ledger."

"Could it have been an inside job?" Amy asked.

"Are you accusing me?" Annika's voice was glacial.

"My family wouldn't do this," Marty said. "And the rest of my staff are like family."

"Amy was right to raise the question. If I were you, I'd find out what happened," Charles said. "Otherwise you're vulnerable to a recurrence.

Also, you'll never really know who you can trust. A hacker is most probably to blame."

"Could you find out for us, Charles?" Marty asked.

Charles appeared thoughtful. "I could run diagnostics for you," he said. "Can you put me in touch with your IT manager?"

"I don't have one," Marty said. "My son, Dan, dabbles in IT."

He was Tim's younger brother, who had joined East West Bridges straight from school. To Kat's knowledge, he had no relevant qualifications. It was a miracle, she thought, that Marty's business thrived despite his disregard for education and training.

"Tell him to call me," Charles said. "In case the problem has infected your other businesses, I'd suggest checking all bank accounts and supplier payments for suspicious activity."

"There's only one bank account," Kat said.

"That seems highly irregular." Charles frowned.

Marty cut the Skype connection.

"Why did you do that?" Amy asked. "It's rude."

"He can't tell me how to run my affairs." Marty stared at the empty screen.

"My dad's just agreed to do you a favour." Amy sat erect in her chair, no longer avoiding eye contact with Marty. A flush rose from her throat to her cheeks.

"He owes me one," Marty said. "I gave you a job, didn't I? I even found a boyfriend for you. Every father wants a good man to take his daughters off his hands."

"I was capable of finding Erik for myself, thank you," Amy said. She flounced out of her seat, glaring at Marty. "You don't need me here anymore, do you? Good."

The heavy wood door slammed shut behind her. Marty wiped a hand across his brow. "Was that a resignation?"

"I don't think so." Kat was sure it wasn't. "Amy needs to cool down, that's all. She was right: it was disrespectful to hang up on Charles."

"He can look after himself," Marty said. "I'll ring him later, and blame the technology. I can't understand what her problem is."

"What century are you living in?" Kat demanded. "This isn't the Victorian era, when women were the property of their men. It isn't even the 1980s. Welcome to the new millennium, Marty."

Like Amy, she wanted to leave his office before she had a major argument with him. Whatever her legal and moral rights, Starshine's profits weren't coming her way any time soon.

Chapter 10.   Charles

"Freddy, I'm leaving at three today. Okay?" Charles suspected it would be, but hated having to ask. Since the mighty Bishopstoke Insurance had taken over his last company, his responsibility and power had gone, along with most of his workload.

Freddy grinned, revealing teeth so perfect that Charles wondered if, like Dee, he'd had veneers applied. The IT director was scarcely older than Amy, a smart young man whose Asian parents had sent him to one of London's top schools. He was too charming to dislike, although Charles's dreary job was another matter.

"You know what I say." Freddy stretched his long, expensively-suited legs. "As long as the work's done, I don't care when you do it."

"Thanks." It maintained the fiction that there was work for him to do.

Charles commandeered one of the quiet booths they were encouraged to use for phone calls. He now had Marty's number among his favourites.

"Are you still on for a meeting at five thirty, Marty?"

"Too right." The Midlands accent was pronounced. "How about the Rose Villa?"

"I think your office is a better bet," Charles said, with a twinge of regret.

Arrangements made, he focused on pulling together a presentation that a layman would understand. With extended vape breaks and a lunchtime pint, it staved off boredom until his departure.

He opted to walk from Blackfriars to Euston station. It was a sunny May day, a light breeze ruffling new leaves on the trees along the Embankment. The Thames Clipper slipped by, leaving a foamy trail on the gently rippling river. A mile away, overlooking the water, was the hotel where he'd expected to marry Dee.

He remembered waiting in vain with the registrar. Dee's glitzy wedding, meticulously planned, could so easily have turned into her funeral thanks to Shaun Halloran's obsession with Kat. Both women had high profiles because of the products they sold; indeed, Dee's name was synonymous with yoga as Kat's was with vodka. They had made a pact with the devil, in Charles's view. The publicity they craved might make them rich, but it attracted too many crazies.

He swerved right abruptly, away from the river and into the Middle Temple gardens. Gothic stone buildings rose from the green like a fantasy film set, or an Oxbridge college transported to the centre of London. Dee's brother, Davey, must have spent three years in such gracious surroundings before leaving Cambridge with first class honours. Gazing at the grand Temple Church, Charles felt a twinge of envy.

He'd grown up too fast, and was paying for it a quarter century later, stuck in a dull job and fearing the axe. Money had lured him to join a bank in London after his A-levels. Others might have worked for a few years and made it to university later, but that hadn't been an option for him. At twenty-one, his girlfriend unexpectedly pregnant with Amy, he'd tied the knot. He was grateful for his pay cheque, then.

That early marriage hadn't lasted. It would be different with Dee. They'd had time to get to know each other first. Amy wasn't rushing to the altar with her young man, either. Perhaps she should. Erik had excellent prospects once his research came to fruition. He was kind to Amy, but rather intense. Charles decided to take him aside when they next met, and explain that he should play as well as work.

The quirky splendour of the scene, and a reassuringly Marlboro-flavoured vape, took the edge off Charles's concerns. He marched past the fringes of Covent Garden and the red brick mansion blocks of Bloomsbury, focusing his attention on the approaching conversation with Marty. Costs and corners had been cut too much. The fraud wouldn't have happened if Marty had employed an IT manager, and a more experienced accountant than poor Annika.

At Euston, Charles bought an indifferent cup of coffee before boarding the fast train to Birmingham. Staring out of the window, he resolved to be tactful. There was no point antagonising Amy's boss.

Of course, the meeting didn't go to plan at all. Marty texted him to say he'd be waiting by the ticket barrier at Birmingham New Street.

"You'd never find your way to my offices," Marty said, shaking Charles's hand.

"I'm amazed anyone finds their way out of the station at all," Charles said. There were at least five exits; he was astonished that Marty had guessed right.

"Fancy a pint?"

"Maybe afterwards. Walls have ears."

Marty nodded. "I think I'll need one. My office it is." He led Charles out of the Grand Central complex, past more shops and bars. It was the rush hour: the pavements swarmed with commuters dashing from work, while cars clogged the roads.

Florence Street was just off a busy highway, which necessitated dodging traffic. East West Bridges itself, and the buildings around it, appeared shuttered and deserted. Only Marty's silver Jaguar sat in the car park, glinting in the late afternoon sun.

"I thought my daughter would be here?" Charles said.

Marty chuckled. "Amy's out the door at five, same as everyone else." He unlocked the door to the spartan reception area, ushering Charles into a large, wood-panelled room.

Charles took a seat. "Any chance of a coffee?"

"My PA's gone home. We'll make that vodka." Marty filled two shot glasses from a bottle etched with twinkling stars. "I want a drink before we start. I don't mind telling you, I wish I'd never gone near darria. It was a money pit even before the theft."

"A good cause, though."

Marty ignored the comment. "Right. Tell me everything."

Charles took a laptop from his backpack, and switched it on. "It's as I thought. A brute force attack through an open RDP port."

"Translate that into English."

"Okay. You have remote desktop protocol enabled, so your employees can do their jobs away from the office. They access systems for logistics, accounts and marketing, to name only three. I explained before that an RDP port is like a door that enables them to do that. Unfortunately, leaving it open exposes you to hackers too."

Marty still looked blank. "You said they forced their way in."

"No, they used a brute force attack to discover the administrator's password for your finance system. Look, here's a list of login attempts. I downloaded it from your server yesterday." Charles pointed to his screen.

"Fifty successful logins and more than six thousand unsuccessful ones?" Marty goggled at Charles's laptop. "I need more vodka." He gulped the shot in one, and poured another.

"Exactly. Look at the times as well. The unsuccessful attempts were during the night, and made rapidly, one after another. It's evidence that a computer program was used."

"Who did it?"

Charles grimaced. He was surprised it had taken Marty so long to ask. "I don't know. All I can tell you is that the IP addresses were either in the UK or Bazakistan."

Marty nearly fell off his chair. "You're not joking, are you?" His face grim, he filled his glass for the third time.

"And breathe, Marty." Charles made a show of inhaling and exhaling. It was a method Dee tried, not always successfully, to moderate his stress. "The Bazakistan connection doesn't mean you were deliberately targeted. It could be pure coincidence. The hackers may not even be located in Bazakistan. I'd put money on it that they are, though. We're seeing a lot of cyber fraud originating in Russia and the rest of the former Soviet Union."

"What about the UK IP addresses?"

"I reckon they're a botnet." Charles saw that he needed to explain. "That's a network of computers controlled by one person, who could be anywhere in the world. The UK PCs might have been infected with a virus, so their owners would be unaware they'd been harnessed to the will of a third party."

Marty downed his vodka. "All bets are off. I haven't got any money. They've robbed me of nearly half a million. I worked my socks off to earn it, and it's vanished at the click of a mouse. By the time I told the bank, they couldn't get it back. And you're telling me you can't either, because you don't know which of the twenty million people in Bazakistan did it? I have my suspicions."

Charles assumed Marty was referring to Kat and Erik's mother. "You'll need proof before you accuse Marina Aliyeva."

"It's too much of a coincidence. She wants her hands on the darria research."

"Amy mentioned that," Charles admitted. "I thought Marina was a socialite, hobnobbing with the President's son. That makes her an unlikely hacker, if you don't mind me saying."

"I'm sure she can find a tame computer nerd," Marty said, adding quickly, "No offence."

"None taken, but I wouldn't jump to conclusions."

Marty took no notice. "How do I stop her helping herself to my bank account whenever she wants?"

"You've already changed all the passwords, haven't you?"

"First thing I did."

"Good. You should make certain they're strong and unique; otherwise, change them once more. Also, ensure the server denies access to users if they make more than three unsuccessful login attempts within twenty-four hours. And check server logs to see if anyone is doing so."

"Got it," Marty said.

"There's more. Use a virtual private network, or VPN, for remote access. It's an extra layer of security."

"Sounds expensive."

"It's not. Mind you, no safeguard is 100% effective. Sorry." Charles held up his hands. Hackers were clever. They learned new tricks all the time. Marty had to be vigilant, especially if he was right about Marina. Even if her hand wasn't on the keyboard, it could be directing someone more computer-literate. "Whatever you do, spend money on those IT basics at least. Skimping on them is a false economy. I hope I've convinced you."

"Thanks for taking the time to help." Marty seemed stunned.

"Don't mention it. It was good to use my brain. Freddy rarely allows me the opportunity."

"Why don't you leave? Isn't the City of London a mecca for cushy IT jobs?"

"I'm waiting to be paid off."

"I'm glad you're not my employee," Marty said. "On that note, let's go to the pub."

He insisted on taking Charles in the Jaguar, although their journey ended in a backstreet boozer so close they could easily have walked.

"Black Country beer," Marty said, sipping a jet-black porter. "Like it?"

"Yes, an honest pint." Charles trusted Marty to choose his real ales. "I'll ring Amy in a minute to see if she's free for a bite before I go back to London."

"A long day for you."

"I'd rather get back to Dee than stay over." In any event, Charles would be expected at Bishopstoke at nine the next morning, regardless of the lack of tasks to occupy him.

"When's the wedding?" Marty evidently saw from Charles's face that the question had hit a nerve, for he followed up with, "Angela wanted to know."

"I'm sorry to disappoint your wife. I'm trying to persuade Dee to keep it low-key this time."

It was proving to be a battle. Dee had the cash for the dream wedding she'd always wanted. It would be a networking event as much as a party, with the great and the good invited to mingle. Dee even planned to be a matchmaker: half a dozen lovelorn friends were on her hit list, including her brother, Davey.

Charles shook his head. "Naturally, Dee still wants a glitzy bash with a meringue dress and champagne on tap."

"Sounds like fun," Marty said. "Who's winning?"

"I will, even though I haven't yet." Charles was determined. "She wants to show the public she's bounced back. Her view is that, when they see her shiny life, they'll buy more yoga courses."

"I can't fault her logic. My wife's completely taken in by Dee's PR spin. Angela watches Dee's online yoga courses every day."

"It's how you sell Starshine too, isn't it?" Charles said. "Only last week, I saw Kat on TV, wearing a designer dress and talking about the rise of craft vodka."

The reality was, he knew, that she spent most of her life managing a factory on a Birmingham industrial estate.

"True," Marty agreed. "Your Amy's idea. She should be proud of herself."

Charles reserved judgement on the wisdom of placing Kat in the spotlight. He acknowledged the impact on Marty's finances. "Amy said your vodka sales have never been better. The theft is a setback for your business, but it hasn't sent it under."

Marty swivelled his palm in a gesture of uncertainty. "I can't pass the business to my kids in this state. When am I ever going to retire?" he said bitterly.

Chapter 11.   Ben

Ben placed his top-of-the-range Alienware laptop in the padded pocket of his backpack. He'd be travelling light, as usual. Once he added T-shirts, underwear and a few dinky-sized toiletries in a clear plastic bag, he'd be good to go. Checking he had his passport before he left, he jumped at the sound of the entry buzzer.

His phone pinged at the same time. Its screen revealed a uniformed policeman staring at the doorcam outside, two floors below Ben's central London flat. Tall and broad-shouldered, a dark monobrow dominating his craggy face, Kyle Lassiter was easy to recognise. They had both attended the same school in London's East End. Although they hadn't been buddies, Kyle accepted that Ben wanted to defy family tradition and stay on the right side of the law. The cop had never paid a social call before and there was no reason for him to start. What did he want?

"Come on up, Kyle." Ben spoke into his phone before tapping a combination into it.

The policeman's only movement was to hold up a hand to the camera. "Are you alone?" he asked.

"Yes." Watching Kyle move inside the building, Ben was even more puzzled. He unlocked his front door, holding it ajar and waiting on the threshold for his visitor to emerge from the lift.

Whooshing and clanging announced the policeman's arrival. His peaked cap adding to the sense of height and bulk, Kyle seemed to fill the lift lobby.

"I just need a word in private." Kyle, expression serious, motioned to Ben to let him inside the flat and close the door. "Oh, you're packing. Where are you going?"

"Prague. A gaming convention. I'm sure it's hosted there because conference halls and beer are both cheap." Most of the delegates would spend too long in the former to take advantage of the latter.

"I assume you're in with a chance of a prize? Go easy on the beer."

Ben nodded. "I won't indulge until I know I've won."

He was keen to display his prowess at Guardians of the Dark Skies, the latest video game to dangle a six-figure prize for its new European champion. There were only two serious contenders for the cash: Ben himself, and an eighteen-year-old challenger from Germany. The young lad had nearly beaten him at a tournament last year. Ben was expecting an interesting game, but he was sure he'd retained his edge.

"I was just passing through the area and thought I'd share some intel. Word's out that your brother's not happy with you."

Ben almost burst out laughing. He'd expected Kyle to tell him something he didn't know. "I'd worked that out," he said.

"He's really, really unhappy," Kyle said. "Have you seen him recently, or any of your family?"

"No." Without an invitation from Jon, Ben couldn't visit his brother in prison. The rest of his extended family hadn't been in touch, and after they'd cold-shouldered him at his father's funeral, Ben had no inclination to make contact with them.

"Watch your step, Ben," Kyle warned. "Jon blames you for your old man's death. I hear he's telling his mates he wants to take care of you personally."

"He's inside."

"And I hope it'll be for a long time." Kyle shrugged. "But you never can tell. He'll be out later this year if the CPS can't make that murder charge stick."

Ben knew little about the case, which involved the killing of a cannabis grower who had apparently double-crossed Shaun Halloran. Jon, ruthless and violent, would have wanted the man dead, even if his own hand hadn't been on the knife. Refraining from revenge would signal weakness. It was naïve, Ben now realised, to imagine Jon wouldn't want to avenge his father's death too.

"Anyway, you can't be sure another chancer won't decide to help Jon out," Kyle said. "He's a powerful figure in prison; involved in all sorts of rackets. Someone may want to earn a gold star. I suggest you stay away from Jon's friends. Even your own family. Got it?"

"Thanks." He appreciated Kyle taking the trouble.

"You're welcome. I'll see myself out."

The door clicked to a close behind him. Ben's legs wobbled. He slumped onto the squashy brown leather sofa. Taking a deep breath, he looked around him.

The rented studio flat was in a prestigious area, and pleasant, but he wouldn't miss it, or his treasured Golf GTi, if he moved abroad. Video game companies were fighting to bring him on board as a brand ambassador. Bankrolled by his employers, he'd have a luxury lifestyle travelling around the USA and Asia, far away from the Halloran clan and their allies.

There was little to keep him in London except his friends at the gaming café he frequented in Hackney, a routine that was well-known to Jon and thus too risky if Kyle's intelligence was right.

Ben was about to sling the final items into his backpack, when his phone rang. A frisson of excitement gripped him as he recognised Amy's number, dissipating as he recalled their last meeting. While they'd been for drinks together a couple of times, Amy had made it clear she wanted a platonic friendship only. She already had a boyfriend. It was a shame. Ben enjoyed her company far more than that of the fangirls who clustered around him at eSports competitions. Still, they were more flexible in their affections than Amy. He appreciated that, at least. When he attended a fixture, he never had to return to his hotel room alone.

There was no time for a long chat, which was all he could expect from her. Ben hesitated. Curiosity, and the memory of her auburn hair and laughing eyes, persuaded him to accept the call. "Amy? I've only got five minutes, I'm afraid."

"Are you in London, Ben? My father's getting married today at the registry office in Camden, and Erik won't go with me. He's got a business meeting he thinks is more important. Can I see you for a drink later?"

She sounded stressed and annoyed. He could imagine her grimacing, twisting a coppery tendril around her fingers.

"Sorry," he said softly. "I'm on my way to Prague for a tournament."

"Bad timing." Her tone was regretful. "Good luck, Ben. Keep in touch, yeah?"

"I will," he promised.

Perhaps he should stay in London. If Amy was cross with Erik, Ben might stand a better chance with her than he'd thought. But was it worth risking his life?

Chapter 12.   Marty

Angela simpered at Marty across the white damask-clad table. "Fancy a Buck's Fizz?"

"For breakfast?" Marty groaned. "I'm in London to work. You have one for me. I'll get pie-eyed later, once I've met the merchant bankers. Anyway, as you're off on a spree with my credit card, shouldn't you lay off the booze yourself? I don't even know why you need new clothes."

"Cruisewear." Angela said, smugly. "Why are you so grumpy? Anyone would think the capital was outside your comfort zone."

"It isn't, but it's not a pleasuredome either." He liked to travel in and out of the Smoke as swiftly as possible, evading the noise, exhaust fumes and extortionate hotels. Enjoyable as it was to spend time with Angela, she had expensive tastes. It was scant comfort that the bill for their stay would be dwarfed by the bank's stratospheric fees.

He ordered more coffee, keen to be on top of his game when he met the City sharks. They'd approached him a month ago with the news that at least three companies were keen to buy Darria Enterprises. A multi-million pound bidding war was likely to result. Marty had been sufficiently interested to insist Erik attended an initial meeting about it, which unfortunately and unavoidably had clashed with Charles's wedding. Erik was in a severe Brownie point deficit with his girlfriend as a result.

Perhaps that was why Erik hadn't taken Amy to London and stayed with her overnight at her father's place, as Marty had expected. Instead, the scientist was catching the milk train from Birmingham this morning.

Usually reliable about time, Erik was late. Marty fumed, weary of making small talk with the bankers. He had nothing in common with them, resenting their public school accents and huge fees. They had lured him with fabulous bait, and now he was dangling like a small fish at the end of the line, they would move in for the kill.

As he waited, annoyance gave way to anxiety. It had taken some cajoling, and the threat of withdrawal of funds, to persuade Erik to engage with the bankers at all. Now, Marty wondered if his business partner had changed his mind. Erik's arrival, thirty minutes into the meeting, induced a surge of relief.

Seeming to sense friction, Erik apologised profusely for problems on the Tube. Marty suspected the bankers never went near the Underground. Expense account taxis were more their style. There were three of them in the room, all white, half his age and exuding an air of upper crust entitlement. It irked Marty that he needed them too much to display the contempt they deserved.

"No worries, Erik, we've got all day," Marty said. "Guy, David and Ash have hinted at good news, but they waited for you before sharing it."

Guy, his black sideburns and waxed hair matching the dark cloth of his three piece suit, smiled. His brown eyes had a predatory glint. "It is good news indeed. We've received an offer of six million pounds from a company called Wellangle."

It was a bland, corporate name, not one Marty recognised as belonging to a global pharmaceutical company. "Never heard of them," he said. "How about you, Erik? You know the players in the industry."

"Wellangle isn't one of them." Erik's tone was sceptical.

"We checked them out," Guy said. "They can afford it."

"They've tendered on a cash-free, debt-free basis, and it's subject to due diligence." David behaved like Guy's shadow: of similar appearance, he would only comment after his boss had spoken.

"Entirely normal," Guy added.

That was stating the obvious. Marty hated to be patronised, but bit his tongue. "The business is in the red, so I accept we won't get the full six," he said. "What were the other bids?"

Ash, thin, blond and effeminate, looked uncomfortable. "The other bidders withdrew from the process."

"That's right," Guy said, sharply. "Once they'd signed non-disclosure agreements, we shared certain financials with all three interested parties. Two indicated they wouldn't proceed to the next stage."

"They felt the recent fraud was a complicating factor," David echoed.

Marty silently cursed Marina Aliyeva. Still, the amount on offer was excellent for a product whose value rested largely on hope. Although they were selling darria herbal tea to defray the cost of the cancer research, the business was still a drain on his resources. Disposing of his investment would release capital to give his children, as well as bankrolling Angela's wardrobe.

"Where does that leave me?" Erik asked.

"Pardon?" Ash said.

Guy pursed his lips. "Glad you raised that, Erik. The purchaser wants you to stay on board for two years, and their bid is actually conditional on that."

"How much control will I have over marketing and pricing?" Erik's body language was wary. "I want this cancer cure to be accessible to patients across the globe, not just developed countries."

Marty held his breath. He admired Erik's altruism up to a point. If it stopped this deal happening, they might not stay friends.

"We can write those safeguards into the sale agreement," Guy suggested, to Marty's surprise. "The bidder should be receptive to it. Wellangle's owners want the broadest possible distribution for the drug."

"May I ask who they are?" Erik said.

"We're required to keep it confidential," Guy replied.

It was probably another client of Guy's bank, and they'd be collecting two sets of deal fees. That would give Marty leverage to pay less. While he liked to see the whites of a man's eyes when he did business with him, more valuable still was the chance to cut Guy's bill. "When can we get this deal signed?" he demanded.

"It's nearly June, and the start of the holiday season," Guy said. "That might slow it down."

Marty imagined Guy spending the whole summer on his yacht in the Caribbean. "So when, exactly?" he asked.

"September is doable," Guy said. "Do you agree, David?"

"Oh, yes. Well before Christmas."

Marty relaxed. His share, even of a reduced price, would be more than two million pounds: the best festive gift he'd ever had. "Then you'll invoice us in this financial year, I suppose?" he said, his manner jocular.

He saw from glances passing between the bankers that he'd hit the mark.

"I want to keep my shares," Erik demanded. "I've told you before that I've got reservations about Big Pharma. I don't trust them. You can sell up, Marty, but I need to be sure I can influence the direction this business takes."

Guy's hungry eyes narrowed. "A partial share sale isn't on the table, Erik."

"Then tell me exactly who owns that company," Erik challenged. "I'm not selling anything or working for anybody I don't know."

Marty glanced out of the window at the glass towers of the City, where trillions of pounds were made from financial wizardry rather than honest toil. He tried to disguise his impatience. This would be a long day.

Chapter 13.   Kat

Kat stared, thunderstruck, at Marty's PA. "Tanya – your hair!"

"I know," Tanya's plump fingers stroked her silver bob. "Going grey gracefully is a shock to my system."

"It was pink a week ago."

"Everyone is, these days. I've had to go back to my roots to make a style statement. Anyhow, excuse me barging into your distillery. Marty would like a word."

Kat grimaced. Now Marty had moved his offices and warehouse into the unused buildings next to her distillery, he was far more prone to interfere in her work. "I can meet him at three. The excise man is visiting this morning, and I've got a delivery of bottles at two." She was proud of Tim's design for Starshine vodka bottles, an etched glass pattern with stars that glowed under ultraviolet light.

"Marty won't like that," Tanya said. "He asked to see you now."

That was too bad. Kat was soon absorbed in her tasks, so busy that she skipped lunch and still scarcely made it to Marty's office on time. Just as she rounded the corridor towards it, he dashed through the door and straight at her.

"Out of the way, Kat. Someone's stealing my car."

She gaped as he dived past her into the lobby where Tanya multi-tasked as the company receptionist.

Kat heard Tanya shrieking. "Don't go out there, Marty."

It was enough to send Kat racing after him. Marty was outside, jumping into the passenger seat of his Jaguar. The door flapped and rattled as the sleek silver car moved forward, heading for the open gate to the road. Suddenly, the vehicle veered to one side, clipping the metal gatepost and coming to a halt.

Marty emerged, his face red with anger. "He's out cold," he said. "What are you staring at, Kat? Call the police."

Kat found her voice. "What happened?"

Marty raised his eyes to the heavens. "What does it look like? This crook was trying to make off with my Jag. I only laid a single punch on him. It was enough."

He marched around the car, pulling a scrawny, denim-clad blond youth from the driver's seat. The lad lolled in his arms, eyes open but unfocused. Pale and spotty, he looked about sixteen. Marty dumped him,

70

none too gently, on the tarmac. His lips tightened as he inspected the damage to his vehicle. Its bumper had cracked and buckled.

Tanya appeared, a small red case in her hand, shock written on her face. "I'm glad you stopped him, Marty. I've brought the first aid kit. I thought I'd need it for you." She knelt by the boy, taking his pulse.

"Don't waste your time on that scum," Marty said grimly. "When he wakes up, the first thing he'll do is pull a knife on you. He tried it with me, even as he stepped on the gas."

That, and the knockout punch, explained why the Jag had swerved off course, Kat realised. "How did he get in your car?" she asked.

"Who knows?" Marty's expression was icy. "Here's my guess. He'll have had a cloned key. I don't how he came by it, but once he had it, all he needed to do was hang around until he gained access to our car park. He was able to do that because someone left the gate open after your bottle delivery. What's the point of securing this place like Fort Knox if you breach our safeguards like that? Well?"

Kat's mouth felt dry. She followed his gaze to the perimeter fence, a high, spiky metal stockade. It should have been impregnable. "Sorry," she said.

"This place is a rathole," Marty said. "I shouldn't have moved my HQ from Florence Street."

"You didn't say that last year when you told me to make vodka here," Kat pointed out.

Marty ignored her. "Has anyone called the police yet?" he demanded, glaring at Tanya as she manipulated the youth's limbs.

"I'm putting him in the recovery position," Tanya said, calmly. She rose to her feet. "Right. That's done. I'll dial 999."

"Sharpish," Marty commanded. "I'm staying out here to make sure our new friend doesn't jump up and do a runner. Kat, I wanted to discuss the sales forecasts. Tanya's printed some documents and left them on my desk. Ask her to find them for you, then come back."

"You want our meeting in the car park?" Kat asked. The sky had darkened. A breeze cut through the humid June air, fanning her ponytail as a warm raindrop hit her forehead.

"No one will overhear," Marty said. It was true that no passers-by were in sight; outside the rush hour, the industrial estate had little traffic and virtually no pedestrian footfall. "Get a brolly if you must."

Tanya was sitting at her reception desk, speaking into a headset, when Kat returned to the lobby. She mouthed 'brown file', seeming to divine what Kat wanted.

Kat smiled back. She retrieved her umbrella from the distillery. Retracing her steps, she entered Marty's office.

It smelled of coffee. Apart from that, and the view of the car park, it had little in common with the room he'd occupied in Florence Street. The heavy maple and leather were gone. Angela and Tanya had chosen the décor, giving Marty white walls, a brace of soft blue sofas, and pale birch furniture. Framed Starshine Vodka posters added accents of colour. Kat had heard Marty complain it looked like a dentist's waiting room. If it hadn't been for the absence of a fish tank, she would have agreed.

She headed for his desk, a curved sweep of light wood. A buff-coloured A4 folder sat beside a notepad. Her eyes were drawn to the words Marty had written on the jotter: 'Marina Aliyeva'.

What was Marty's connection with her mother? He hadn't bought vodka from her for nearly two years, refusing to touch it again once he'd detected methanol in a consignment. Marina had tried to sue, of course, but that was ancient history as far as Kat knew.

Temptation proved too strong. Kat picked up the notepad. An arrow drawn vertically below her mother's name pointed to a roughly sketched oblong, in which Marty had written 'Johnson – Grand Cayman'. Underneath that, another arrow led to a square, labelled 'Wellangle.'

That triggered a memory. Hadn't Erik told her that Wellangle wanted to invest in his darria research? If Marina Aliyeva was involved, Erik couldn't possibly know – could he?

Chapter 14.   Marty

"It's just speculation, Erik," Marty said. "I don't know for sure that Marina owns either Wellangle or the Cayman Islands shell company." He could feel his business partner's negative energy crackling over the phone.

"Why did you write it down, then? Seems too specific to be a guess."

"It was a doodle." Marty gave up. "All right, cards on the table. I engaged a private investigator to find out who was behind Wellangle. She contacted me to voice her suspicions, but I wanted documentary proof before I spoke to you."

"When will you get it?"

"Soon. Can you understand why I didn't say anything? I knew you'd be unimpressed."

"Noted." Erik sounded more conciliatory.

"Do me a favour, Erik. Tell your sister not to snoop around my office." This was all Kat's fault. Why had Tanya let her spy on his personal papers? He'd have words.

"I'm not selling anything to my mother."

"Nor am I, Erik." As he said it, Marty realised to his astonishment that it was true. Whatever riches Marina Aliyeva offered, it wouldn't be enough. She had the blood of at least one true friend on her hands.

The call having finished amicably, Marty jabbed his phone to begin another. He formed his lips into a false smile, his pride deterring him from requesting assistance, but his brain overriding it.

The young car thief was making a fuss about being hit and suffering concussion. He claimed Marty was the aggressor. No doubt his lies were aimed at securing compensation.

Kat and Tanya were witnesses, but how reliable were they – especially Kat? Marty had enough on his plate dealing with the aftermath of the fraud and now the difficulty of finding someone outside Bazakistan to buy the darria business. He didn't need a long, public legal case as well.

The phone was answered. Marty began to call in favours.

Chapter 15.   Charles

Freddy had crashed out of his twenties with a birthday party at the weekend. Summoned to his office on Monday morning, Charles noticed the first grey hairs sparkling in his boss's oiled black thatch. Freddy's brown skin had paled and there were bags under his eyes.

"Not your first hangover, I assume?" Charles said.

"Definitely my worst." Freddy groaned. "The timing's terrible. HR messaged me as I was on my way in. The board want to outsource our IT to Poland."

Freddy made it sound as though the decision had suddenly dropped from the sky, without input from him. Charles doubted that was the case.

"I want you to plan our transition to the new regime," Freddy said.

Charles swallowed. He would be busy for the first time in six months, when all he wanted was a pay-off. "I can draft an outline, but you'll need a trained project manager after that," he suggested. The company already employed a few of them. To his knowledge, they did even less work than him.

A project manager's salary would be lower, too, and it was obvious that Freddy realised this. "I can't keep you on for long, then, Charles. You're looking at a redundancy package."

Charles hid his triumph. Once the meeting was over, he went outside for a vape break. With the approach of midsummer, the sun was blazing on his favourite spot overlooking the Thames. Although a public place, it felt more private than the open plan office where he whiled away his days. Charles allowed himself to enjoy the surge of nicotine in his bloodstream before phoning Dee.

"Put the champagne on ice, darling. I've finally got the brown envelope."

"Has Davey spoken to you?"

"Your brother? No. Why?"

"His new girlfriend's given him a job, and he wants you to work for him again."

"I'll call him."

Freddy could hardly sanction him for spending a few more minutes in the fresh air. Charles strolled further along the riverside, enjoying the view of sunlight glittering on the Shard. Finally, he tapped his brother-in-law's number.

"Charles! Just the man. Still bored at work?"

"About to be un-bored. Freddy wants me to move the IT function to Poland."

"So the IT team will hate you instead of him? Clever." Davey laughed. "Listen up if you'd rather do something more exciting. Jeannie has asked me to run her business empire, and we need an IT director. As well as having a great boss, you'd like the company's mission. We're planning a series of ethical investments."

"You're talking about Jeannie, who you met at my wedding last month? Quick work." Charles couldn't decide whether to be more impressed by Davey, or Dee for her matchmaking.

Davey didn't comment on that. "Can I count you in?"

"Show me the colour of your money."

"I'll match your current package, plus 20%. Now, tell me what you know about Marty Bridges."

Chapter 16.   Ben

It was another courtroom. In the market town of St Albans, Ben had expected the premises to be both ancient and lax on security by comparison with the coroner's building in central London. He was wrong on both counts. A short walk downhill from the station, his destination resembled a bland modern office: a squarish block constructed of yellow and orange brick. Entering the revolving doors, he was guided to queue for an airport-style security arch.

When Ben walked through, it bleeped alarmingly, as it had for everyone ahead of him.

"Over here." A youthful security guard, neat in white shirt and black trousers, scanned him with a wand. "You're good. Know where you're going?"

"No. I'm here as an observer."

"We have a nice café." He pointed to the rear of the spacious lobby. "Then the courts are upstairs."

"How can I find the right one?"

"You're looking for a particular trial? Just check the screen over there to see where it is."

Jonathan Matthew Halloran and three others were listed under Court 1. Ben saw that the co-defendants were Vincent Mowatt, Scott Andrew Reynolds and Gerald John Aloysius Shanahan. Vince, he knew as Jon's best friend and lover. Jerry and Scott were his father's old schoolmates, viewed by Shaun as disposable foot soldiers despite their shared history. Jon presumably saw them in the same light.

Already late, Ben hurried up the softly-carpeted stairs. Despite mounting apprehension, he noted a scent of polish and a lack of sound. He knew it wasn't necessarily wise to attend the trial. It would draw his family's attention to him again. Unless he could settle his differences with Jon, that was dangerous.

He wanted to attempt a reconciliation rather than run away, though. Coming to the court was his only chance. His presence, day by day, would signal moral support. While he wouldn't be allowed to speak to Jon, he could look him in the eye.

To Ben's relief, when he was finally admitted to Court 1, he found Clive and the rest of his cousins hadn't bothered turning up. He didn't care whether he ever saw them again or not; it was Jon's rejection that hurt.

This case was far less newsworthy than a shootout involving celebrities. The solitary journalist, a petite bottle blonde in her forties, was scribbling notes in the media corner to the left of the public gallery. Ben sat as far away from her as he could.

The sparsely filled public seats were of a space-saving design that had to be flipped open, like those at a cinema. Indeed, there was a sense of theatre about the scene in front of him, not least the costumes of the court officials. Almost a dozen people in black gowns were arrayed on benches in the centre of the courtroom. Half of them sported elaborately curled white wigs. Ben assumed these were the barristers.

The judge wore similar clothes, with the addition of a red cape and purple sash. As the coroner did in London, he sat at a long wooden desk, elevated on a dais. This ran along the left-hand edge of the square chamber. While other walls were simply painted white, this one was clad in cream marble and decorated with the royal coat of arms.

Ferocious air conditioning dispelled any notion of summer heat. Ben kept his leather jacket on. He noted that most of the jury, their benches on the other side of the gaggle of lawyers, had done the same.

The dock, a glassed-off alcove, occupied the right-hand wall. Ben peered across the room, rewarded with a glimpse of his brother. Jon and his wingman, Vince, sat together in the front row, bookended by uniformed security men.

Behind them, another pair of prisoners sat with their guards. Ben barely recognised Jerry and Scott, older and shorter than the distant figures he remembered from childhood. He hadn't seen them often; they'd appeared at the family barbecues his mother used to host each summer.

Her death from cancer had been a watershed for him. She'd never stopped his father's violence towards him, but she'd softened it. Once she was gone, he'd retreated further into video games, fortunately leading to a lucrative career.

He would have given it up to have her back. Now, Jon was the only close family he had left. Ben stared at his brother, hoping in vain to be noticed.

The judge was addressing the jury. "Although Anton Dimmock grew cannabis in a wood outside Dunstable, his remains were found in the garden of Lilac Cottage, a property in the Hertfordshire village of Broxbourne. You will hear it is the Crown's case that Anton Dimmock's death was not accidental, and that he was murdered by the four defendants because he had annoyed Jonathan Halloran's father."

As he spoke, Ben saw that the white woolly wig lent a false impression of advanced years. The judge's face was unlined. Like three of the five bewigged barristers sitting before him, he was probably no more than a decade older than Ben.

The first witness was called, Acting Sergeant Trevor Bryce of the Hertfordshire Constabulary. He walked between the dock and the public gallery to reach the witness box, situated in front of the media section. Jon's gaze swivelled towards him. He spotted Ben at last.

Jon's response was a nod before he returned his focus to the policeman. Ben was quietly relieved to see no indication of anger.

Bryce swore an oath on the Bible before facing the jury. Ben had a clear view of the black-clad policeman's profile. Middle-aged and chubby, he could virtually rest his notes on his protruding beer belly.

By contrast, the prosecution counsel, Mr Good, was rake-thin, young and brisk. "What were you doing on the twenty-second of March 2017?" he demanded.

A chill danced down Ben's spine. It was the date of his father's death.

Bryce replied. "I drove to Lilac Cottage in Broxbourne with PC Christopher Cooper. It was our first job of the morning. We arrived just before nine o'clock."

"Was your visit prompted by the disappearance of Mr Anton Dimmock some months previously?"

"No, it was an unrelated matter."

Mr Good turned to the judge. "Your Honour, although nothing to do with the deceased, I believe the subject matter of Acting Sergeant Bryce's visit is of relevance to the court."

One of the defence lawyers stood up. "I disagree, Your Honour."

"Well, Mr Good?" the judge asked. "I can send the jury out while we debate the issue, if it's important to you. Is it?"

Mr Good pursed his lips. "No, Your Honour. That won't be necessary. I'm sorry, Mr Bryce. Let's continue. Who did you encounter there?"

"The owner, Ms Barbara Fensome, her two children, and her partner, Mr Scott Reynolds. There was another male who was observed running away from the property."

"Who was that?"

"It was later found to be Shaun Halloran, a criminal on the run."

Ben flicked his eyes towards the dock. Jon was staring straight ahead. The only sign of emotion was a red flush stealing upwards across his pale face. He was wearing a suit, shirt and tie. Ben was reminded again of his father's advice.

"Did you see anything out of the ordinary?"

"Apart from Mr Halloran running through the back garden?" Bryce said, to laughter from the jury. "Yes. The family dog appeared, carrying a human bone."

"May I ask how you knew it was a human bone?"

"Certainly," Bryce said. "I have a degree in human anatomy. It has given me some familiarity with body parts."

"Thank you. What happened next?"

"I asked Chris Cooper to give chase to Mr Halloran while I radioed for assistance. I was about to do so, when I heard Mr Reynolds' mobile phone ring."

"Why is that important?"

"He didn't answer the phone, but we established later that the call came from Gerald Shanahan. That gave us a significant breakthrough in our investigation."

"As the jury is aware, Mr Shanahan is also on trial, and we will be hearing from him," Mr Good announced.

Continued questioning confirmed that Shaun Halloran had given police the slip, a fact that came as no surprise. The judge told the court to break for lunch. Refreshingly, the reporter took no notice of Ben as he left the room. He avoided the café and strolled outside into the sunshine, just to make sure their paths didn't cross.

Jerry Shanahan took the stand three days later, a whiff of tobacco and body odour assailing the public gallery as the defendant was brought from the dock. Craggy-featured, bald and podgy, Jerry barely fitted into his grey suit. A blue paisley tie failed to disguise his cream shirt's bursting buttons. Ben supposed Jerry had put on weight in custody.

It wasn't just Jerry's waistline that might cause his doctor some concern. The man's skin was haggard, his eyes suspiciously blackened. He seemed edgy.

Jerry didn't look in Ben's direction. Disappointingly, Jon hadn't done so either since that moment on the first day. Right now, Jon, his face unreadable, had fixed his gaze on the witness box.

This was the first defendant to speak, which meant his lawyer would question him first and Mr Good would cross-examine afterwards.

Discounting the pensioners on the jury, Jerry's barrister, Mr Cullimore, was the oldest person in the room. Wisps of genuine white hair trailed from the wig. Once his client had been introduced and sworn in, he adopted the expression of a kindly old uncle.

"I understand that you were forced to watch a terrible event at Lilac Cottage on Tuesday, the seventh of June 2016?"

"No." Jerry's mouth twitched.

Mr Cullimore raised an eyebrow. "Was it perhaps a different date?"

"No. I didn't see anything bad, then, or any other time."

"I see."

Ben doubted that Mr Cullimore did, but the barrister maintained his confident, sympathetic façade.

"You did, of course, give a statement to the police, suggesting that you brought Mr Dimmock to Lilac Cottage in June 2016, expecting that he would receive a telling off from your co-defendants, only to see them murder him. Is that statement incorrect in some way?"

"It isn't true. None of it. I never met Anton Dimmock in my life. Nor Vincent and Jonathan."

"What about Mr Reynolds? Isn't he your friend?"

"Well yes." Jerry was sweating, a note of hysteria in his Cockney tones. "I know Scottie, obviously. We were mates since school. I've been round to his place for…for a cup of tea. I've never seen anything strange there. No skeletons in the cupboards or convicts in the garden."

"I see." Mr Cullimore remained unruffled. "Why did you make up a story of murder for the police?"

"I had flu. I should have been in bed; the fever was that bad. If I was thinking straight, I wouldn't have said those silly things or said no to a solicitor. I was delirious; I mean, I must have been hallucinating."

Mr Cullimore smiled. "It takes a brave man to do the decent thing and admit they didn't tell police the truth. You are to be commended for that, Mr Shanahan. Of course, you are speaking under oath in this court."

"That's right. I wouldn't lie on the Bible," Jerry gabbled.

"Thank you, Mr Shanahan," Mr Cullimore said. "I have no more questions."

"Your Honour, if I may raise a suggestion?" Jon's lawyer was young and pretty, her skin peachy and her long dark hair flowing in a loose ponytail beneath the wig.

"Yes, Miss Quinn?" The judge beamed at her.

"The only substantive evidence against my client is this so-called confession from Mr Shanahan, and now we hear he's retracting it. Couldn't we save everyone's time by striking the case out?"

Mr Good's face was thunderous.

The judge raised a hand. "I'm sure you have the best of motives, Miss Quinn, and had Mr Shanahan declined to give evidence at all, I would probably have agreed with you. Now he's in the witness box, though, it is right that Mr Good, you and our other learned friends have the opportunity to cross-examine him."

"I shall certainly do so," Miss Quinn said. "And I take it you will remind the jury of the dangers of convicting solely on the evidence of the co-accused?"

"I have every intention of so reminding them," the judge said. "Mr Good, if you would be so kind, do you have any questions for Mr Shanahan?"

"I do, Your Honour."

The language and rituals were far more legalistic than those at the inquest. Ben understood the gist of it, though: Jerry was perceived by the judge as unreliable.

Ben shared that opinion, up to a point. He was inclined to think Jerry's statement hadn't been a lie. Even disregarding the black eyes, he could imagine Jerry retracting every word once he realised a lifetime of prison solitary confinement lay ahead of him. If he went down, knives would be ready for him. For all his youth, Jon was a powerful figure within Belmarsh. His influence would extend elsewhere in the prison estate; convicts would want to please him by sticking a blade in Jerry's back, or ground glass in his food.

Meanwhile, Miss Quinn took her seat again. Her eyes flicked to a laptop in front of her as she made brief notes. Strutting like a bare-knuckle prize-fighter, Mr Good rounded on the hapless Jerry.

It was the seventh day of Jon's trial. The reporter, absent for most of it, had returned. In contrast with her, Ben had sat in the public benches throughout the proceedings. As a succession of witnesses came and went, he'd searched his brother's face for a reaction, but there had been none. Jon remained impassive.

Now, Jon was to speak in his defence. Apart from Jerry, who Miss Quinn had successfully painted as a liar who couldn't be trusted, none of the accused men had ever admitted anything. Scott, who might reasonably have been expected to notice a corpse in his garden, had claimed no knowledge of it. To be fair, the plot was about an acre in size and the bones had been found in an overgrown corner.

Vince had declined to testify, pleading stomach pains. Ben thought he was probably stressed; he remembered Vince as living on his nerves.

Jon, ignoring Ben as he marched to the stand, elected to swear on the Bible. That was no doubt to impress any jurors who happened to be religious. Shaun had raised his boys in the Roman Catholic faith, but neither had adhered to it. It was hardly surprising, given that their father had broken all the commandments without a second thought.

Comely Miss Quinn began by asking Jon when his mother died.

"Seven years ago," Jon said.

"When you were thirteen, then."

"Yes."

"Do you miss her?"

"Objection," Mr Good called. "How is this relevant, Your Honour?"

The judge nodded. "Miss Quinn, do you care to explain?"

"I'm building a picture of the challenges my client has faced in his young life," she replied smoothly.

She was allowed to proceed. Ben liked her style. He was sure that he would also agree with her if, like the judge, he was faced with an onslaught of her charm.

Jon appeared animated at last, expressing sorrow at his mother's death, remorse at being persuaded by his father to carry a gun, and puzzlement at the charges brought against him.

"Did you know Anton Dimmock?"

"No."

"What about your co-defendants?"

"I shared a flat with Vince. My father wanted him to keep an eye on me."

"Your father was not, perhaps, the best judge of your welfare." Miss Quinn sounded sympathetic.

"I see that now." Jon was obviously acting the little boy lost, his blue eyes wide and appealing. "He was my dad, though. I loved him."

"And did you know Scott Reynolds and Jerry Shanahan?"

"Only by sight, as a child. They were at my cousin's christening in 2008." Jon was playing the religious card again. "My dad always said Jerry Shanahan was flaky. He made things up."

Ben doubted his father had made any such comment. He thought hearsay was not supposed to be allowed as evidence. Still, the jury had heard it.

"What do you make of Jerry Shanahan's confession, as outlined by the prosecution?" Miss Quinn asked.

Jon didn't hesitate. "It's a fairy-tale," he said. "Even he says it isn't true."

"Why would Jerry Shanahan lie about you?"

"I don't know." His tone was one of hurt innocence. "I haven't seen him for years."

"Have you ever visited Scott Reynolds' cottage in Broxbourne?"

"No."

"Did you kill Anton Dimmock, as the Crown alleges?"

"No. I didn't know him. I've never been to Broxbourne."

"Where were you on Tuesday, the seventh of June 2016?"

"Vince and I saw a film at Cineworld, I think. X-Men Apocalypse."

"You think. Aren't you sure?"

"Sorry, Miss." Jon sounded boyishly ashamed. "I couldn't know it would turn out to be an important date."

"Of course." Miss Quinn's smile blazed first at Jon, then the jury. "Nobody could possibly have foreseen the sad events of that day."

Nobody except Shaun Halloran, thought Ben. According to Jerry's statement, Shaun had a grudge against Anton and had given instructions from his prison cell for Jon to organise a termination. If the Hallorans were perceived as weak, others would take advantage of them. Shaun would never let that happen.

"Is there anything else you'd like to say to the court?" Miss Quinn asked.

"Only that I regret the mistakes I made in my youth," Jon said. "Carrying a gun was a single moment of stupidity. I'm very sorry and I'm atoning to society by serving my time for it."

"You hadn't been in trouble with the police before, had you?"

"No, and I don't intend to break the law again."

Ben had to hand it to his brother: he was a better liar than Jerry Shanahan. He was sure Jon was running a drugs ring in prison, and had committed many more offences before he went inside. There had always been a tacit understanding that Jon would inherit Shaun's criminal empire; despite his detention, he was doubtless still governing what remained of it.

The spotlight moved to Mr Good. Older and sterner than Miss Quinn, he injected scepticism into his words as he asked, "So, prison has taught you a lesson, Mr Halloran."

"I made a mistake and I'm paying my dues to society," Jon repeated.

"You made the mistake of getting caught," Good said. "And now you've made another mistake, using Gerald Shanahan as part of your crackpot scheme to teach Anton Dimmock a lesson. Do you know the phrase, 'pour encourager les autres', Mr Halloran?"

"It's all Greek to me," Jon said.

A few jurors tittered. Like their counterparts at the inquest, they were a mix of very old and very young adults: pensioners and students. Jury duty was supposed to be for everyone, but Ben wasn't surprised to see that those in the prime of their careers had managed to evade it.

"Your father wanted Anton Dimmock dead, didn't he?"

"I don't know." Jon's voice was composed. The image he presented was nothing like the angry young man in the coroner's court.

"Your father told you to kill him, didn't he?"

"No."

"How did you get to Broxbourne? Train, car, taxi?"

"I've never been to Broxbourne."

"What about your friend, Vincent Mowatt?" Good emphasised the word 'friend', nastily. "Has he been to Broxbourne?"

"You'd have to ask him."

"Yes, or no, Mr Halloran?"

"No, not to my knowledge."

Good tried a different tack. "You claim not to have seen Gerald Shanahan for years, but he seems to know a lot about you. He told police that you and Mr Mowatt travelled to Broxbourne from Tottenham. You and Mr Mowatt did live together in Tottenham, didn't you?"

Again, he stressed the words 'live together'. Despite his differences with his younger brother, Ben seethed. Who cared if Jon was gay? If Good was hoping for a homophobic jury, it was a risky strategy. They could just as easily turn against the Crown for his bigotry.

Jon didn't rise to the bait, anyway. "Jerry Shanahan was a friend of my father's. I expect he'd heard where I lived. I've told you already that I haven't been to Broxbourne."

Good couldn't shake him. Whatever he insinuated, Jon simply denied it. Ben suspected he'd been coached by Miss Quinn, given a swift lesson in the importance of playing to the gallery.

The Crown's case appeared unproven, and no more witnesses would be called. Apart from Jerry's confession, there was no evidence that any of the four had been party to a murder. The cause of death wasn't even clear, as Anton's corpse had festered in Scott's garden for so long that it had been partly eaten by animals by the time it was discovered. Scott's theory, expounded at length to Mr Good, was that Anton must have wandered onto the plot like a stray cat and died of natural causes.

Ben felt that was improbable, but the Crown had to prove its case beyond reasonable doubt, and it hadn't. There was no way the jury would convict Jon. He would still be leaving the court in a prison van today, though, as he was serving time for possessing a firearm. The earliest parole date was December.

Jon was returned to the dock. Conflicted, Ben tried and failed once more to catch his brother's eye. He wanted Jon to taste freedom again, but what if Kyle Lassiter was right? How big a price would Ben himself pay once his brother was released?

Chapter 17.   Erik

"So we have a deal?" Erik said, the Rose Villa Tavern's soundtrack giving his conversation privacy as usual.

"Seems we do," Marty replied. "Once the lawyers dot 'i's and cross 't's, we're in the money. I don't know how long it will take, though. It should be well before Christmas. Ho, ho ho. Even the City slickers can't drag their feet for six months."

"You really think Jeannie Jenner's offer is genuine?"

"I've no reason to suppose not. She's well known as a rich, philanthropic investor. Anyway, she's almost family to you, surely? She's stepping out with Amy's stepmother's brother. Try saying that ten times, quickly."

"I don't remember. I'll ask Amy about her."

Marty winked. "Family gossip – in one ear and out the other? I'm the same when Angela talks about her folks. Guy can get his lawyers on it. Given the exorbitant fee he's raking in, he can stump up for the legal costs. He's paying for a wild party when the deal closes too, that's for sure."

"Wait," Erik said. "I want the paperwork to be absolutely clear. We're both selling our shares, but I'll still have voting rights and a job with Darria Enterprises. Can you get your lawyer to check all the documents Guy gives us, please? I don't trust him."

"Of course," Marty said, to Erik's relief. "You're right. Guy would sell his own grandma." He drained his pint. "Want another, to celebrate? You're going to be a millionaire."

"No thanks." Erik grinned, finally allowing himself to relax. "I'll take Amy out. She'll be delighted."

Marty reached into his wallet, handing Erik a sheaf of notes. "Buy her a drink or three from me. I'm sure Guy didn't find Jeannie Jenner for us all by himself." He stood, clapping Erik on the shoulder. "Have a good night."

Erik tapped at his phone as Marty left, winking at him. The call went to voicemail. He texted Amy, 'Gr8 news! Let's go out. Champagne is on Marty!'

His phone bleeped at once with a reply. 'Sorry, had to go to London for work again. A xxx'

It was as if a bucket of cold water had been poured over him. Erik couldn't understand why Marty hadn't mentioned it.

Chapter 18.   Ben

Ben's inbox was buzzing with birthday messages, but he'd only received one card. There was no need to guess who had sent it. Jon's name and prisoner number were carefully inked on the back of the envelope.

Time appeared to stop. Ben's hand trembled. He'd been frozen out of his brother's life for so long: his presence at last month's murder trial ignored, his letters unanswered. He wondered if this was a threat or a cheery missive.

Although it wasn't yet noon, he took a beer from the fridge, downing the bottle in one. He reached for another, swigging as he finally tore open the envelope.

The greetings card bore a picture of Batman. The legend 'Now You Are 6' had been changed to twenty-six, the number 2 inserted with a blue ballpoint pen. Inside, the same writing said, 'Have a gud day, Bro. Come see me soon. I told Clive to back off of you. Jon.'

Hope filled Ben's heart at the green shoots of a reconciliation. Perhaps Jon's mood was more positive now he'd beat the murder charge. The short note was as much as he could expect. Jon had hated school, unlike Ben, who had managed a year at university before his mother's death drove him further into the fantasy world of gaming. Shaun had seen no sense in books or learning, and his favoured son felt the same.

Ben drained the dregs of his beer in celebration. Regretfully, he left the rest in the fridge, locking his flat and descending to the basement garage to collect his black Golf GTi. Minutes later, he'd parked it outside his favourite gaming café in Hackney.

In mid-July, the schools hadn't begun their summer holidays yet, but GCSEs and A levels were over. Although it was the middle of the week, the place was packed. His friends, older and quieter than the pheromone-scented adolescents, grumbled about it. Like Ben, they had been gaming for more than a decade. He realised it didn't occur to them that they, too, had been spotty and irritating once.

He slipped into the seat his friends had saved for him, turning around again as a cheer rose throughout the room.

"Ben – surprise!" One of his fangirls, a sixth former, was carrying a tray of chocolate brownies, a lit candle wobbling precariously on the cake in the centre. She was beaming with pride, her long dark tresses and round face gleaming in the flame.

Ben made a show of huffing and puffing to extinguish the fire. There was a hail of applause before she led everyone in a chorus of Happy Birthday.

"Thanks, Brittany." He was flattered she'd made such an effort, but he didn't want to gush.

"I thought you'd like it. They're home-made." She served him a slice, thrusting her T-shirted chest forward. Her brown eyes reminded him of a puppy.

Ben accepted his tribute. "What are you playing today?" he asked, only half hoping she'd take the hint and return to her PC.

Brittany was much too young, and if he was honest, too chubby for him. His ideal woman was slender Amy, hair fiery as his birthday candle. Unfortunately, she wasn't in town, and Brittany was right in front of him.

Chapter 19. Marty

Marty had drummed a work ethic into Tim, Dan and Martha by employing them as soon as they left school. Milly, his youngest, was a lost cause. She flitted from one job to another, appearing to spend more time in Birmingham's cocktail bars than she did working. He was disappointed, but not surprised, when she was late.

"I rang her at eight this morning to offer her a lift," Tim said. "She didn't want one."

"How did she sound?" Dan asked.

"Hung over."

"You don't suppose she went to Florence Street?" Martha suggested.

"She'd find a heap of rubble if she did," Marty said. "It's only October and the site's already been flattened. No, she must know where we are, what with her fiancé working in Tim's sales team. When Callum whispers sweet nothings to the bab, surely he'd say his job's moved to Aston?"

"Yeah, right," Martha muttered. "I'll ask Tanya to track her down."

It was ten thirty, half an hour after the scheduled start of the meeting. Sensing an atmosphere brewing, Marty resolved to give Milly fifteen minutes. After that, he'd explain to the family why he'd called them all together, whether she was there or not.

Apart from leaving school early, this was the biggest decision he'd ever taken. Marty forced himself to make small talk about football while his eldest daughter was out of the room, raising an eyebrow when she returned with a coffee pot and cups.

"Isn't that Tanya's job?" he asked as Martha flicked back her long, fair ringlets, and began to pour drinks.

Martha sighed. "She's gone off on her Yamaha to fetch Milly."

"Has Milly ever ridden a motorbike?" Marty asked.

It appeared not. Milly dashed into the room in a state of excitement. "That was fun."

"I bet," Marty agreed. "I've had bikes, back in the day. Still would, if Angela was up for it. I've had a BMW, a Triumph…"

"Really?" Milly's eyes glazed over. "Not like Tanya's, Dad. You should have seen us whizz through the bus lanes. Sorry I'm late. My car broke down."

"Not near here, I hope?" Marty asked. "They'll have the wheels off soon as look at it."

"On the ring road." She jerked a thumb behind her. That didn't fill him with confidence, but if harm befell her small Skoda, it might teach her to maintain it better. At twenty-eight, it was about time she learned.

Now, with four curly blond heads facing him over the circular birch table, Marty had his children's full attention. "Wondering why you're here?"

"It's like the scene in the film where the lawyer reads the will." Dan grinned. "The only difference is, there's no lawyer, and you're not dead."

"And I don't intend to be any time soon," Marty said. "However, to make sure the taxman doesn't get more than his fair share, I have to give away my assets while I'm still breathing." He paused, gripped by indignation at the thought of HMRC taking any tax from him, alive or dead.

"What do you have in mind?" Tim asked.

"An equal split. You'll each receive a quarter of my shares in East West Bridges and in Starshine vodka."

There were smiles from Dan and Martha, worried frowns from Tim and Milly. Milly had presumably twigged that she'd be Callum's boss. Her boyfriend did whatever she said anyway, so Marty couldn't see a problem.

"Kat owns half of Starshine." Tim sounded puzzled.

"Right. My half will be divided four ways, so you Tim, and your brother and sisters, will own one-eighth each of the total." Marty scanned his children's faces for signs of unease, thankfully seeing none. He'd agonised over Starshine himself. The smart new vodka had more potential for growth than his old East West Bridges distribution business. Now, Tim and Kat would control Starshine between them. While he couldn't rely on Kat to play fair, he trusted Tim to treat his siblings honourably.

"You're really letting go? We'll be running the business ourselves?" There was hope in Tim's voice.

"Yes." Marty was reassured he'd made the right decision. He hadn't appreciated Tim's eagerness to pick up the reins.

"What of the other JV, Darria Enterprises?" Tim asked.

"Good news," Marty said, "but it's between these four walls, please. Erik and I are selling our shares."

"Kat hasn't said anything." Tim's eyes narrowed.

"I'd hope that she didn't know. It's confidential." Marty had signed undertakings to that effect. He had just breached them. "Please don't tell anyone. It's been in the air for months, and I expect the sale to go through any day, certainly by the end of November. It removes a millstone from my neck, and yours. It means I can give you each five hundred grand in cash as well." He couldn't take it with him, and he'd have plenty left for a comfortable retirement.

They were still processing the information. Marty fell silent, waiting for the inevitable questions. His children would have to agree between them how to manage the business and whether to invest their newfound wealth in it.

Milly spoke first. "When can I have the money? The sooner I get a new car, the better."

Chapter 20.   Kat

"Sure you want me to taste-test these?" Tim asked, eyeing the new ready-mixed cocktails with concern. "I'm a beer drinker; I don't have the palate for them."

"Yes, but you know what sells," Kat told him. "We'll use Marty's office. He's out."

Tim grinned. "That will be my office soon."

"Don't get too attached to it. It's the largest room in this industrial unit, so it makes sense to have all our meetings there. You should redecorate as well. You're handy with a paintbrush. Let's have an edgy vibe rather than the boring corporate look."

She gathered a collection of small bottles, placing them on a tray. "Ready?"

Tim nodded. He was more easy-going than Marty. Kat sensed she'd face less of a struggle for resources than in the past. She caught herself daydreaming about a bigger copper still. Three years before, the images drifting through her mind would have been designer dresses.

They left the functional laboratory, a glass-walled space carved out of a corner of the distillery. Tim hailed employees as they passed the distillation equipment and then through the warehouse, stacked high with cartons and crates. Kat noticed a subtle change in her co-workers' attitudes to him. Before, despite being Marty's son, he had been accepted as one of them. Now, as the CEO in waiting, he was management. False smiles and an absence of banter greeted them.

Having persuaded Tanya to bring water and glasses, Tim sat at Marty's birch meeting table. He stretched his legs. "Right. What have you got for me?"

"Seasonal Bellinis. Spring, summer, autumn, winter." Kat began pouring the sparkling drinks.

"With prosecco, no doubt."

"Absolutely."

Tim's eyebrows arched upwards. "Do I detect Angela's hand in your latest idea?"

"She may have been involved," Kat admitted. "We've had a few drinks together recently. She's still keen to host our wedding in her back garden next year."

Tim winced. "That's kind of her, but Dad's retirement changes everything. You and I will be busy. We won't have time to organise a fancy wedding."

A sudden chill gripped her. "Are you saying you don't want to get married?"

"Not at all." Dismay was written on Tim's face. He rose to his feet, enveloping her in a hug, lips brushing her head.

His mouth moved swiftly to hers. "Where's your passport? Let's just fly somewhere hot, and do it. We don't need to impress anyone," he said, between kisses.

"Not this side of Christmas." Kat suspected he was right. There was no need for a meringue dress and a huge, polite party to impress distant relatives. She didn't have a family, anyway, apart from Erik. Her estranged mother would never be invited.

She needed time to think about it, though. Tempting as the notion was, she couldn't abandon the distillery in November, when production was at its peak.

"Vegas gets my vote," Tim said. "You used to be a croupier. Check out the swanky casinos."

"Just remember the house always wins," Kat said. She'd have to ensure he set a limit and stuck to it. There was a risk that, swayed by the glamour of the gaming tables, he'd lose his inheritance. She'd seen it happen to punters; indeed, she'd played a part in persuading them.

Tanya knocked on the door. "Do you want coffee?"

"Yes, and biscuits please," Tim called. He turned to Kat. "Ah, the power."

She giggled. "I feel like a child playing at being grown up."

Tim's eyes twinkled mischievously. "Mummies and daddies? Later."

Tanya arrived with a cafetière, cups and shortbread. "Your brother's been trying to call you, Kat. Do you want to give him a bell before you start on these?"

Tanya's bossiness was so understated that Marty never noticed it. Kat stifled a chuckle, while appreciating the hint.

"I've left my phone in the lab," she told Tim. "Can I use yours?"

"Be my guest." He found Erik's number in his iPhone, and handed it to her.

Erik answered at once. "Hi Tim, what can I do for you? Any idea where Kat is, by the way?"

"It's me," Kat told him.

"Have you heard the news?" Erik sounded excited.

"No. I've been working all morning."

"There's been a coup in Bazakistan, or at least, an attempt. The President is indisposed, with heart trouble, after a spiked drink. His son, the head of the secret police, is acting President while he recovers."

"His son? Our mother's special friend…"

"According to Marty," Erik interrupted.

"I thought you believed every word Marty says." Kat laughed without mirth. "Still. Isn't this convenient for her?"

Chapter 21.   Erik

Erik's cheap Motorola smartphone buzzed constantly. The Bazaki expat WhatsApp group was going into overdrive with rumours about the coup. Half of them mentioned Marina Aliyeva's name. A smaller subset pointed out that her second husband, Arystan Aliyev, had died of heart failure: surely no coincidence. It was pure speculation, although most observers didn't admit that. They were silent, too, on the sole death for which Erik held Marina accountable with certainty: that of his father, Alexander Belov.

More worrying were the reports of an un-named fifty-six-year-old woman in police custody. That tied in with his mother's age. Tension gripped him, and he told himself not to panic. There must be thousands of females in Bazakistan who shared the exact date of her birth, let alone the year. Surely it couldn't be Marina?

He had to find out. She'd killed his father, robbed Marty's company, tried to whip away his darria project from under his nose, but she was still the woman who had given him life.

He had two telephone numbers for Marina: one for her home, the other her cell phone. Neither was answered. After trying several times, he phoned her distillery in Bazakistan. They would know if she was in trouble.

Despite more than a decade in exile, his command of Russian remained fluent. The switchboard connected Erik to Marina's secretary. Her response only amplified his sense of foreboding.

"Marina Aliyeva? She's not here."

"Where is she? Is she safe?"

"It's not possible to say."

"Is there someone in authority I can speak to, please?" He felt sick with exasperation and anxiety.

"I'll put you through."

He didn't know who would be taking the call, and nearly fell off his chair when a deep voice announced, "Tolya Aliyev speaking." This was Anatoly, the eldest of her second husband's illegitimate children.

"It's Erik White."

As far as Erik knew, Anatoly and Marina detested each other. Anatoly's next words confirmed it. "I've heard of you. The murderess's son."

Erik saw no point in denying it. "Yes. Do you know where she is?"

Anatoly laughed, a sound that had nothing to do with humour and everything to do with triumph and revenge. "She's in jail."

"Why?"

"Need you ask? There has been an attempt on the Old Man's life." He added conversationally, "She succeeded with my father, but not this time. Now she will pay for her crimes, and I have been given charge of my father's distillery at last."

Erik refrained from mentioning that it had been his own father's distillery in the first place, and Arystan Aliyev had acquired it by dubious means. "I thought you were an oil services engineer, not a vodka maker," he said.

"I understand how everything works. There are good people running the plant, and I watch them closely."

The engineer would have to be careful. His distillery had produced poisonous vodka before, although perhaps that had been Marina Aliyeva's intention all along.

Erik recalled that Marty, who was mostly a good judge of character, thought well of Anatoly. The engineer might give him more information about Marina's plight. "Tolya, Marina was responsible for my father's death. Did you know that? She betrayed his political leanings to the authorities. They sent him to the north, to a labour camp. When he didn't die quickly enough for them, they shot him. Then she was free to marry again. I'm sorry that didn't end well either."

"And I'm sorry for your loss, too." Anatoly sounded as if he meant it.

"Where are they holding Marina? Have they farmed her out to the gulags?"

"Not yet. There's been no trial, has there? She's in the grey box."

Eric shivered. This was the high security jail attached to Kireniat's central police station, a Soviet-era concrete cube. Its few windows were tiny squares, inset just below the roof. Most cells had no natural light.

As the owner of a distillery, Marina had enjoyed a life of luxury. The privations of prison would be a shock, surpassing whatever she'd suffered during Soviet times and the early, famine-stricken years of Bazakistan's independence.

It was possible she would never leave the grey box alive. "I have to see her," Erik said.

There was a pause. Eventually, Anatoly spoke. His voice was strained. "You won't get her out. No bribe could be big enough to save her. Given what she's done, I'm sickened that you'd even try."

"You misunderstand," Erik said, trying to stay neutral. It wasn't worth taking offence. Anatoly didn't know him well enough to appreciate that corruption wasn't his style. "When my father was taken into custody, I was a student, powerless to help or even return to my country. I never said goodbye to him."

"So you want to say a fond farewell to Marina? You're a fool. Don't waste your time."

Chapter 22.   Kat

"You did what? You're insane." Kat couldn't believe it.

"I fly out tomorrow," Erik said.

"Don't get involved. She doesn't deserve it."

"Blood is thicker than water, Kat."

"She doesn't think so, does she, or else why betray our father?" Kat stared at her phone, wishing Erik was standing in front of her. She would grab his shoulders and shake sense into him.

"She's a patriot," Erik said. "She loved her country – our country – more than her husband."

"And her children."

"Exactly. She gave up everything for Bazakistan. In that, our mother has been consistent. So whatever she's done now, it must have been at the behest of the state."

"How could it have been? Take a reality check." Kat didn't bother hiding her frustration. For all his fine intellect, her brother was being extraordinarily dense. He still thought fondly of their mother, while she couldn't bear to utter the word. "Marina Aliyeva tried to kill the President. The state wouldn't have commanded her to execute its ruler. I don't know why she did it, and I don't care. As far as I'm concerned, she attacked the Old Man fifteen years too late. If she'd had any love for our father, she'd have done the deed decades ago – and done it properly."

"Either she didn't do it, or she was following orders," Erik said. "It's completely out of character otherwise. Don't you see, Kat? She's innocent of wrongdoing."

"Just this once?" Kat's laughter was hollow. "I don't buy it. Anyway, thanks to her, our father's dead. Want to bet he's her sole victim? My guess is not. All you know is that she isn't Mrs Popular in Bazakistan right now. You understand that means we're not Master Popular and Miss Popular ourselves? You'll be putting your life at risk. Remember what happened when I went back to Bazakistan? You told me not to go, and you were right. I was kidnapped."

"In other circumstances, I wouldn't return, but she needs me. I have to make sure she's okay. Whatever it costs. I can borrow money, get her the best lawyers. I'll pay it back once the sale of Darria Enterprises goes through."

"That sale's not guaranteed. Who's going to lend you anything?" She was playing the devil's advocate. Erik wasn't the only one waiting for that money. She had Tim's share earmarked for distillery kit. Any left over would pay for the deposit on a house.

He was being uncharacteristically stubborn. Erik was usually inclined to compromise. It explained how he worked amicably with Marty, while Kat found herself exasperated at the businessman's controlling attitude. Used to twisting her older brother around her little finger, she was reaching the end of her patience.

"What does Amy say?" Desperately, Kat wondered if Amy could change Erik's mind. She'd have to work on her first, of course. Obviously, Erik's girlfriend must have given her blessing to this ill-advised trip; he surely wouldn't have booked a ticket otherwise.

"It's got nothing to do with Amy," Erik said.

Her beloved brother had closed every avenue except the road to Bazakistan, and certain danger.

Chapter 23.   Erik

Kat's reaction was hardly unexpected, but it didn't stop Erik mulling over her words. She was right: he must tell Amy. The trouble was, Amy would agree with Kat. They would both try to stop him. He wouldn't put it past Amy to hide his passport.

To make sure she couldn't, he left the ground floor office, dashed up two flights of stairs to his attic flat, and retrieved the document. Hastily packing a suitcase, he checked if he could switch to an earlier flight.

He would ring Amy when he was far away, too far for her to interfere. Guilt needled him. His girlfriend would be upset. It was too bad; his mother's welfare was more important. For now, Amy would have to manage with a note. He began writing it, expressing his love in a way that, somehow, he'd always found difficult face to face.

Then, he rang Tim.

"Erik, what are you doing? Kat's going up the wall."

"My father's dead." He tried to explain. "I'm the man of the family now, and I have to make sure Mother's okay. Look after my sister – please."

"You'll be dead too. Don't do it."

"I have to go. Promise me, Tim."

"You know I'll do anything for Kat."

"Thanks." Erik cut the call.

Chapter 24.   Marty

"You're joking. At least he's not on the way to the airport yet." Marty nearly dropped his phone. For once, he agreed with Kat. He found himself promising her he'd put all his plans for the day on hold until he'd spoken to Erik.

Kat's brother didn't answer his call. Marty made his excuses to the customers he was allegedly entertaining. They were spending the day at a motorbike exhibition on the outskirts of Birmingham.

"Sorry, something's come up."

"It always does, Marty. You're never going to retire."

"Isn't that the truth?"

Would Erik survive his trip to Bazakistan, and would Jeannie Jenner still buy the darria business if he didn't? Marty had plenty of time to ruminate on his dark thoughts. Seeing the sluggish lines of traffic at the exit to the conference centre's car park, he left the Jaguar there. It would take an hour to drive to Erik's office. He'd save time by catching a train; there was a frequent service to New Street from the railway station nearby.

The fifteen minute journey through the suburbs dragged as he worried for Erik's safety in Bazakistan. Marty had made countless business trips there, ready to use his fists in the early days, and pay commissions to the right people. The only time he'd feared for his life was when freedom fighters had kidnapped him. He was virtually certain Marina had masterminded that, although she'd had a shock when she discovered Kat had been abducted too.

Erik's situation would be more perilous. His card was already marked, as he'd refused to move his research to Bazakistan. Now his mother was in jail, he would be considered a traitor's son. There was a real risk that Erik, like his father, would simply disappear.

That fear alone would have curdled Marty's stomach, but it was coupled with apprehension for the future of the darria plans. Marty had an agreement in principle with Jeannie Jenner's company, but no contract had been signed for the sale. She was unlikely to be impressed if the brains behind the cancer cure walked out of the door, never to be seen again.

There would be legal wrangles over Erik's shares, too. Who would own them if he died? Marty suspected it would be Kat. Worse still, if no one knew whether Erik was alive or dead, title to the shares would remain in limbo. Unable to sell to Jeannie, Marty would be left running a research project he neither understood nor could afford. Jeannie's cash would stay in her bank account, rather than funding his retirement and nest-eggs for his children.

He jabbed at his phone repeatedly, still failing to reach Erik. Finally, the train rattled through unlovely industrial estates, passing the imposing new Birmingham City University buildings and diving underground to halt at a dingy white platform. Above, the glitzy Grand Central complex persuaded shoppers like his wife to part with their money. At this basement level, Marty saw the same New Street station he had known all his life: a 1960s warren crying for a lick of paint.

He ascended escalators to the modern glass bubble above, marching outside to the tram stop. It was quicker than walking to the Jewellery Quarter, or taking a cab around the roadworks. Boarding a tramcar, he scowled impatiently until it glided past the shops, bell ringing.

The grand frontages of the Jewellery Quarter's Victorian red brick workshops were elaborately decorated with terracotta mouldings. Erik lived and worked in a cobbled alley snaking between the sides and round the back of such properties. Here, the walls were more modest: brick cliffs, three storeys high, occasionally punctuated by small, barred windows.

The building was right at the end of Leopold Passage, where the winding lane opened out into a courtyard. Marty had keys for both the front door and the open plan office just inside it.

"Seen Erik?" he asked the sole freelancer he found there.

"He went home." The young woman pointed to the ceiling.

Marty dashed back to the lobby and up the sweeping staircase, taking the steps two at a time. On the top landing, a pair of locked doors faced each other. One gave entry to Amy's bedsit and the other to Erik's slightly larger apartment. Marty banged his fist on the latter.

"Erik – open up!"

"What's that noise?" Amy emerged from her studio.

"Do you know where he is?" Marty demanded.

"On a plane." Tim, his mouth set in a grim line, stepped past Amy.

Now, Marty saw Kat standing behind them, her eyes red and puffy from crying. She turned her head away at his glance.

"He left me a note, there." Amy pointed inside the flat. A sheet of A4 paper lay beside a teddy bear on her white lace-covered bed.

Marty was not too distracted to notice the toy. In any other circumstances, he would have teased her about it. "What does it say?" he asked, gently.

"He's gone," she said, her face pale. "Erik changed his flights. His plane's already left Birmingham for Schiphol, where he'll get a connection to Kireniat. It's a dangerous place, isn't it?"

"I won't sugar-coat it. In Bazakistan, you can't afford to be careless." Marty shook his head, trying not to let fear infect him.

"I'll phone a friend," he said. The only problem was, he didn't really have any left in Kireniat. Marina, the black widow, had despatched two trusted business partners to their deaths. Anatoly Aliyev, son of the second, was his only hope of saving the son of the first.

Chapter 25. Erik

Kireniat, Erik's birthplace, had changed in the last fourteen years. Ritzy glass towers dwarfed the Bazakistan city's Soviet-era apartment blocks. The rolling mountains in the distance, the street names and the old landmarks remained.

A surge of recognition overwhelmed Erik as Anatoly Aliyev's white Mercedes whisked him to a hotel. Here was the café where he drank tea with his first girlfriend; there, hugging the rosy dawn sky, a snow-tipped peak where his father had taught him to ski. His mother, pregnant with Kat, had been waiting with hot drinks when they returned from the slopes.

A wave of love and fear for his mother caught his throat. Tasting bile, Erik realised the city was also calling to him. He hadn't expected that, and hardened his heart to it.

He was ignoring his pinging mobile phone, too. Upon landing at Kireniat airport, he'd seen the brief message from Marty informing him that Anatoly would meet him. There was a link to a business website with Anatoly's picture. Erik had sent a note of thanks, then texted Kat and Amy to tell them where he was. There was nothing more to say.

"I still think you're crazy," Anatoly said, amicably. He spoke in Russian, as he'd done from the moment he stepped in front of Erik in the arrivals hall.

Erik refrained from asking him why he was prepared to help. In this treacherous place, any friendship was precious.

"No comment?" Anatoly's saturnine face broke into a smile, illuminating grey-blue eyes beneath the mane of black hair that matched his smart suit.

Erik sighed ruefully. "I've hardly slept. I changed planes at Schiphol and Riga." Unlike Marty, who travelled business class, he'd bought an economy ticket. It wasn't cheap, though; walk-up fares generally weren't. The last leg of the flight, overnight, could have provided a chance to slumber, but the seat was too cramped. Erik had dozed restlessly.

Anatoly stopped at a red traffic light. "What did you imagine would have happened if I hadn't met you at the airport?" he asked, his eyes peering intently at Erik's.

"I would have caught a bus downtown, to my hotel. I booked it already, online. Marty's mentioned the place often enough; it's comfortable and cheap."

"Wrong," Anatoly said.

"What do you mean?"

The lights changed. Traffic ahead of them resumed the stop-start rhythm of rush hour.

"I mean," Anatoly explained patiently, "that the police would have been waiting for you. They have the manifest; they know who is arriving on each flight. You would have been taken aside before you reached a bus stop or taxi rank. I have a friend at the station, and he is a useful ally to have. He told me this when I enquired after your mother's health." His face darkened.

"How is she?" Erik suddenly felt wide awake.

"They're not treating her badly, if that's what you think. Don't imagine I care." Anatoly sounded bitter. "I asked if you might be permitted a visit, and the answer is yes, when my comrade is on duty. That will be at two this afternoon. Want to come back to my flat first, and grab some rest on the couch? I doubt your hotel room will be ready yet."

Erik weighed up his options. He'd gain more respite at Anatoly's apartment than in a hotel coffee shop. "Sure. Why not?"

Anatoly took a sweeping left turn onto a wide boulevard of black poplars. The trees were still in leaf, although their colour was changing from emerald to gold. They nearly obscured the low-rise buildings behind them: ranks of ornate yellow and white mansion blocks, four storeys high. At the end of the street, Anatoly swivelled the car around, almost doubling back into a service lane. The vehicle halted abruptly.

"I live here," he said. "There's a car park in the basement, but I'll be driving straight to work after this. I'll be back later to take you to the grey box." He jumped out of the Mercedes, opening the passenger door for Erik and fetching his suitcase from the boot as a taxi driver might.

Entrance to the block was via glossy black double doors, each with a tiny, head-height window crossed with fancy wrought iron bars. To the left, a wall-mounted pad listed the occupants in neat black Cyrillic handwriting next to a set of buzzers. There were buttons for the numbers 0 to 9 below. Anatoly punched in a combination, and with a click, they gained access.

Inside, there was a spacious, but dark, hallway. Sunlight seemed to soak into the black-tiled floor and the walls and ceiling, which were panelled in a chestnut wood echoed in the rising staircase. "I'm on the first floor," Anatoly said, flicking a switch to reveal a dim bulb high above.

"I'll carry my own suitcase." Erik scanned his surroundings. The property, obviously once occupied by the Soviet elite, was neat and clean, all wood highly polished. He clumped up the steps after Anatoly.

The engineer's apartment appeared little bigger than his own, tidy and minimalist, its living room wall painted a bilious green. Anatoly guessed at his thoughts.

"Not as grand as you expected? My wife and four sons have a horse farm outside Kireniat. She doesn't want me around now the boys are grown up. It's an old story. These days, I live for my work."

"As do I," Erik said.

Anatoly's eyes narrowed. "No girl on the scene? A man your age should be settling down. Take a tip from me, when you find one, be sure to pay some attention to her. They like that." He gestured to the only substantial piece of furniture in sight, a tan leather sofa positioned opposite a wall-mounted television. "Please. Relax. You'll find a kitchen and bathroom through that alcove, and a bed if you really need it. Help yourself to any food and drink you want."

Anatoly left, locking the apartment door behind him. Erik yawned, his eyelids already beginning to droop. He stretched out on the couch, letting sleep claim him at last.

On the plane, his over-active mind had chewed over nightmare scenarios involving his mother, bullets and torture. Now, he was so fatigued that nothing disturbed him until Anatoly returned.

"Wake up." The engineer stood above him, grinning. Bright midday light filtered through the leafy trees outside, casting dappled shadows into the room.

"What time is it?"

"One. You've been in dreamland for four hours. Want something to eat?"

Erik nodded.

Anatoly vanished into the alcove, reappearing a few minutes later with a robust wooden tray, large enough to require a handle at each end. He set this on a narrow table, unfolding two dining chairs next to it. "Come. There's rye bread, cheese, apples and tea."

Erik gratefully spread sheep's cheese on the black bread. "Quite a nostalgia trip."

"I should think so. All burger and chips in London, isn't it?"

"They don't make tea properly." Erik had always enjoyed the ceremony of brewing leaves on top of a samovar, drinking the pungent liquid with lots of sugar. He poured a mugful from the proffered china pot. His muzzy head and aching limbs began to ease. Finally, his brain was functioning again. Images of his mother floated into it, and he shuddered.

"The vodka plant's working well, seeing as you ask."

"Glad to hear it," Erik said politely. "I'm not a distiller myself. Medical science is my field. It's my sister who's continued our family tradition."

"Ah yes, Kat and her Starshine vodka." Anatoly's blue eyes were frosty, his mouth tense. "I've seen photographs."

Erik grasped the implication. "Kat may look like Marina, but she's not the same person. She isn't interested in politics. The work she's doing now is what she's always wanted."

"She obviously exercised her charms on Marty, because he's buying all his vodka from her rather than us."

Erik couldn't begin to explain Kat's uneasy relationship with Marty, and didn't want to. "Marty had supply problems. Were you aware of them? Your plant despatched vodka contaminated with methanol a couple of years ago."

"I'd heard." Anatoly grimaced. "It won't happen again. I'm an engineer, the same as my father. I may not have trained in the industry, but I understand that safety isn't optional. You can assure Marty that quality will be tightly controlled from now on."

"I'll let him know," Erik said, feeling uncomfortable at the direction of the conversation.

"Do that. We could use those export sales. Since Marina stole my inheritance on my father's death, she's run it into the ground."

Erik couldn't fail to appreciate the irony. Kat had been raised to believe the Snow Mountain distillery on the edge of Kireniat would be

108

hers. That had changed with their father's death, and the transfer of the business to Arystan Aliyev, a dubious transaction that Kat had tried to fight in the Bazaki courts. It was only once she realised she'd never wrest Snow Mountain back from Anatoly's father that she'd decided to develop Starshine.

"Shouldn't we be going now? It's nearly two o'clock," he asked, apprehension mounting as he pictured Marina in a grim prison cell.

"Of course. Leave your suitcase. You can collect it later." Anatoly returned the tray and crockery to the kitchen. There was a brief sound of running water.

Erik pulled an anorak over his leather jacket. It looked warm outside, but it was a time of year when the temperature dropped suddenly in his homeland. It might be dark when he emerged from the visit. He didn't know how long he'd be permitted to stay with his mother.

"Ready?" Anatoly led Erik from the apartment and back to the Mercedes, which was parked a little further down the service road.

"Nice Merc," Erik managed to say, finally alert enough for small talk. As he couldn't afford to run a car, he was by no means an expert. His acquaintance with Marty had taught him that drivers of luxury vehicles were proud of them, however.

Anatoly glowed. "I think so. The E-Class Estate is their best." He opened the passenger door and waved Erik inside.

Morning's traffic having dissipated, the drive was short and smooth. Anatoly steered into an underground car park below a modern complex of shops and offices. They took a lift to the surface level, emerging on another street.

"There," Anatoly said, pointing to a 1960s concrete oblong across the road.

Even if he hadn't recognised the police station, Erik would have known it by the rows of striped cars in front of the building. Like sentries, they lay both within and beyond the black metal stockade which served to keep the public at bay. As he watched, two officers strode through a gate, rifles slung across their shoulders. They took one of the vehicles, which sped away, sirens blazing.

"Wait," Anatoly said. "I'll tell Max we're here." Removing an iPhone from his jacket, he tapped the screen. There was a brief chat, as a result of which Max was waiting at the gate by the time the pair had jaywalked across the busy road.

"Good to meet a friend of Tolya's." Max opened the gate, then held out a hand.

Erik shook it.

Smart in his peaked cap and white shirt, Max looked to be about the same age as Anatoly, although his sandy hair was greying and his amiable features vanishing into fat. He wasn't carrying a rifle. Instead, Erik's eyes were drawn to the belt holster of Max's black uniform trousers.

"You'll take Erik to Mrs Aliyeva. Let's have a coffee while he's there," Anatoly suggested.

"Fine. Hang around in the waiting room for a few minutes," Max said. He used a card to gain admission through the front door. This led to a shabby, cream-painted corridor, its drab linoleum floor gleaming with polish yet still appearing dirty. To the left was a reception counter behind thick glass, and to the right, another passageway. Max shepherded them through this, consigning Anatoly to a square chamber.

Erik glimpsed easy chairs occupied by nervy-looking men in trim suits. Anatoly waved, unconcerned at being left in such company. They were probably lawyers. Erik would have to find a suitable representative for Marina, but he wanted to talk to her first. He wondered what Anatoly and Max would discuss. Was this when a bribe would be delivered? He was perturbed at the notion that he might be in Anatoly's debt.

"Ready for the grey box?" Max asked. "It's at the back." He didn't wait for a reply, but wove through a warren of corridors, several of which required him to use his access card again.

Eventually, they reached another reception area. This was guarded by two of his colleagues: younger men with pistols in their belts. They were playing cards together. At Max's approach, they twitched to attention.

"I bring a visitor for Marina Aliyeva," Max said.

"He isn't booked in." The policeman sounded bored.

"I've agreed it with Leo."

"Why didn't you say?" The man's ratty face peered suspiciously at Erik. "I can give you ten minutes."

"He'll need longer. Shall I ring Leo...?"

"No, no. All right. Twenty; no more. Follow me."

"I'll come back for you then," Max said. "If you want me earlier, just phone. Here's my number." He gave Erik a business card.

"There's no signal in the cells," the guard said. "Come on then." He pointed ahead of him.

Here, there was no lino, or paint, just bare concrete punctuated at intervals by metal doors, each with a letterbox-sized observation slit. There was a strong smell of disinfectant, although fluorescent lights picked out dark stains on the floor. Erik tried not to think about them. He marched down the long, claustrophobic passage, ignoring muffled noises from the cells, concentrating on the echo of his footsteps.

"This one."

At the guard's words, Erik stopped. He'd walked straight past Marina's door. Turning, he saw the man take his keys and open it with a grinding sound.

"Inside. You will be locked in."

Erik stepped across the threshold between freedom and captivity, seeing his mother for the first time in two years.

Marina Aliyeva was wearing black jeans, sweatshirt and flat pumps. The combination emphasised her long blonde hair, creamy skin and petite stature. There was no make-up on her face, yet she was still pretty, wearing her years lightly. At his approach, her green eyes sparkled with joy. "Erik!"

Chains clanked as she rose from a concrete bench to air-kiss and hug him. Her touch was gentle, as if he were a delicate piece of china. There was the faintest whiff of Chanel. Despite her embrace, the atmosphere in the windowless cube seemed ten degrees chillier than in the corridor outside. A cockroach peeped out of a crumbling crack, then scuttled back again.

"How did this happen?" He pulled away and gestured at the dismal environs.

Marina winced. "It's a long story."

"Tell me."

"It begins just after I last saw you in London. I was summoned to see my boss…"

"The Old Man's son?" Erik interrupted.

"His favourite, yes. We call him the Young Chief."

"I see." Erik knew this; it was a term used in the WhatsApp group.

"So. He's rarely in Kireniat. They sent an official limousine. I expected to go to his office in the capital, but instead, it was a ski lodge in the mountains. The reason, apparently, was that he was afraid of listening devices."

Despite the severity of the situation, Erik laughed. "He's the head of the secret police, and he's scared of being bugged?"

"We have plenty of colleagues who know how to do it," Marina said crisply. "When I tell you what he asked of me, you'll understand the need for privacy. He wanted me to hasten the President's death. The Old Man's mental faculties are declining, yet he wouldn't resign or nominate a successor."

"So the Young Chief thinks he should be the Crown Prince? Has anyone told him that republican rulers aren't dynasties?" This was exactly what the rumours in London were hinting.

"This story will play out, but I won't be around to see the finale."

Erik blanched. She couldn't be serious. "No. I'll get you a lawyer. We'll create a media storm: tell the world what's going on. There has to be a way to get you out of here."

"In a wooden box," Marina said, her tone resigned. "My usefulness is at an end. I failed in my orders: I didn't bring the darria research to Bazakistan, and I didn't put the Young Chief on the throne. If I speak the truth, he'll deny everything. Erik, when they write my confession for me, I'm signing it."

He gawped, horrified. "Don't give up."

"You have to know when to stop. If I resist, it's a ticket to torture. My best hope is a swift show trial and the firing squad."

"Like my father, then."

"As you say." Her eyes softened, and looked away. When they returned to him, the affection on her face had hardened to determination. "I've accepted his fate, and my own. Don't make it yours too. You must go back to London now, Erik. Take the first plane anywhere. It doesn't matter where, just get out of Bazakistan."

The rough grey walls seemed to close around him, entombing them both.

"Please go."

He didn't want to ask more questions. What was the need? He held her in his arms once more, clinging to her, remembering how he'd done this as a toddler and wanting to savour the moment now, so he recalled it in future. Her cold metal chains were solid enough, but his mother already felt frail, insubstantial as a ghost.

"I love you," he whispered.

She stood on tiptoe to kiss his cheek. "Goodbye. I love you, too, and Katya. Please tell her."

Erik nodded, knowing Kat would scoff at the sentiment. It was senseless to divulge that to his mother. Nausea clutched at him as he considered her doom and his lack of power to avert it.

A guard banged on the door. "Time's up." he said.

Erik released his hold on his mother. Leaving the cell, he waved cheerily at her. She blew him a kiss in exchange. Their eyes met for the last time.

"Didn't you hear me? Move." It was the other jailer: young, thin and spotty. He reeked of cheap tobacco. Locking the door behind Erik, he led him to the desk where poker hands lay splayed on the scabby wood surface.

His rat-faced colleague looked up.

"Leo wants to see you," he whined.

"Your boss? Why?"

The lad stared at Erik as if he were mentally deficient. "We ask the questions."

Although alarm surged through him, Erik maintained an impassive expression. He forced his shoulders to relax.

"Very good," he said. "Let's not keep him waiting."

The lad exhaled sharply, as if he'd been expecting a fight. Erik followed him back to the labyrinthine office area of the police station, which now seemed light and airy. They ascended two flights of stairs. Halfway along another passage, Erik's guide stopped outside a handsome oak door, on which a brass plate bore the name 'L Denisov'. It reminded Erik of visits to Marty's workplace. Status symbols were evidently the same the world over.

The guard knocked on the door. It was opened by a frazzled-looking woman of middle years, her olive skin betraying Bazaki rather than Russian origins. Her tight magenta dress flattered her trim figure, if not the dyed red hair scraped back in a bun. "Yes?"

"It's the Englishman, Dinara," the lad said.

"You may go, then." To Erik, she said, "Come in." Her kohl-rimmed eyes regarded him shrewdly.

Dinara obviously carried out the same function for Leo as Tanya did for Marty. Leo's PA occupied a cramped cubbyhole furnished with a pine desk, table and two typists' chairs upholstered in orange. The tools of her trade were neatly laid out: laptop wired to a pair of extra screens, notepad, pens, samovar, mugs, spoons, tea and sugar. Post-it notes sat in colourful rows on a pinboard, beside a crimson raincoat hanging from a hook on the wall.

"Please." She gestured to an open door. "He's waiting for you. Would you like tea?"

"Thank you." Erik smiled at her, causing her face to light up in return. Tense lines gone, she was revealed as younger than he'd first thought.

"I'll bring it through."

"What does he want with me?"

The moment of comradeship passed. Dinara's gaze was fixed on the samovar. "That's for him to discuss."

Erik halted by the door, taking a deep breath to keep his emotions in check. A mixture of curiosity, fear and loss threatened to overwhelm him. Finally, he entered Leo's room.

Just as Dinara's workstation was reminiscent of Tanya's, Leo operated from an office like Marty's old quarters in Florence Street. It was designed to impress. Ten times the size of Dinara's anteroom, it was lined and furnished in oak. A traditional wool rug, patterned in squiggles of red and gold, covered the ubiquitous linoleum. Leo lounged in a horsehide swivel chair, his feet on the splendid leather-inlaid desk before him. He didn't rise for Erik.

"You're Erik Belov?" Leo spoke Russian with a hint of the countryside in his accent. His cold blue gaze swept over Erik. The face beneath the cap was youthful, yet hardened. As boss of the station, Leo was powerful, and it looked like he enjoyed it.

"Erik White." Erik extended a hand.

Leo didn't take it, instead pointing to a less luxurious seat opposite. "Of course, your allegiance lies with the Queen of England," he sneered, as Erik sat down.

"How can I help you?" Erik asked, ignoring Leo's contemptuous tone.

"You've offended people in high places," Leo said, bluntly. He removed his feet from the desk, and leaned forward. "You're using the nation's indigenous herb, darria, for the benefit of an English pharmaceutical company. It's a theft of intellectual property from Bazakistan."

Erik sensed colour rising in his cheeks. Whatever he'd expected Leo to say, it wasn't this.

"It's not true," he said. "I don't know who's making that claim to you, but it's risible. No one in Bazakistan paid any attention to darria, until I'd spent years studying it and researching its properties."

"A professor in Bazaku City is working on it," Leo said.

"Maybe now that I've obtained a patent and almost finished clinical trials." Anger sent the words tumbling out. "If this goes to court, I'll win. You know that, don't you?"

"It won't go to court." Leo paused. Frost glittered in his eyes. At last, he said, "I'm empowered, on the President's behalf, to place restrictions on your movement. You will stay in Kireniat, Bazaku City, or points in between. You will transfer the business of Darria Enterprises to Bazakistan."

"I can't do that, because I don't own the business. Marty Bridges has half the shares. Anyway, you have no right to detain me." A disquieting notion formed in Erik's mind: that it had been a trap all along, and his mother was part of it. Raging with indignation, he nevertheless wondered if he'd been too hasty when he noted Leo reaching into a trouser pocket.

"You're a citizen of Bazakistan, Mr Belov." No pistol had appeared yet. Leo's hand was still.

"Not anymore. I have a British passport."

"Let me see it." Leo stretched his other arm across the desk.

Erik handed it to him.

"Thank you." Leo smirked, fetching a cigarette lighter from his pocket, and flicking it on. He applied the flame to a corner of the burgundy-coloured document. Bitter smoke rose as the edges blackened and curled.

Erik jumped to his feet.

"Sit down." Leo's voice was pure ice. "You're in trouble. Don't make it worse."

Chapter 26. Marty

"He's in the grey box with Marina? Why, Tolya? What did he do?"
Marty stared, unseeing, out of his office window. Hoping he'd misheard,
he clamped the phone to his ear, listening over a backdrop of static.

"He did nothing," Anatoly Aliyev said. The line hissed and crackled.

"Tolya, Skype me over a VPN," Marty advised. "I'll text you my
handle." He didn't want the Bazaki secret police snooping on their
conversation.

Beer was his usual tipple, but he felt drawn to a stiff shot of Starshine
from the bottle he kept for visitors. He swallowed it in one mouthful
while he waited for Anatoly's call.

His IT security had been considerably tightened, with Charles's help.
Marty now used a VPN with his iPhone, iPad and laptop. So, he hoped,
did everyone else in his business: he'd certainly ordered them to do so.

Anatoly was back in contact within minutes. "Much better," Marty
purred, relieved at the lack of background noise.

"As I was saying," Anatoly began, "it's not so much what Erik has
done, as what he hasn't done."

"You're talking in riddles."

Anatoly cut to the chase. "Word's out that the government wants Erik
to conduct his darria research in Bazakistan. They're holding him
prisoner until he agrees."

Marty whistled. "Darria Enterprises is my company too. There's no
way I'd agree, so what then?"

"Indeed, what then? I am guessing, Marty, that research will grind to a
halt without Erik to supervise it. I would also propose that the Bazaki
state authorities realise this. They may gamble that you would rather give
them a slice of the action than see your substantial investment vanish
altogether."

"Marina Aliyeva is behind this, isn't she? Her arrest was a ploy to lure
him to Bazakistan."

"No. I wouldn't be sitting in the distillery manager's office if that was
the case. She's not long for this world."

Good riddance, Marty thought. "We have to get Erik out. I'll contact
the Foreign Office. What's the worst that could happen? The Bazaki
authorities won't kill Erik. They may deny all knowledge of his
whereabouts, I suppose."

"That's very likely."

"Any other suggestions, then?"

Anatoly appeared to have lost his voice. Eventually, he said. "It's difficult. The hardest part is getting him released from custody. They want him to sign documents first, and he's refused."

"Good man," Marty said.

"If he wasn't in jail, getting him out of the country would be easy," Anatoly mused. "Bazakistan has a long land border, as full of holes as a Swiss cheese. The police are trying to keep smugglers out, rather than hold anyone in. If you want to leave without fuss, you head for the mountains."

"How passable are they, with winter on its way?"

"If Erik sticks to the valleys, it's okay for another week at least. But to get him to the border in the first place, we have to prise him loose from the police." Anatoly sighed. "It wasn't a problem to arrange for him to see Marina Aliyeva. It cost me a couple of bottles of vodka for Max. I'd willingly do that for a friend, Marty, and I count you in that number."

Should he be flattered? Marty suspected he knew what was coming next.

"This time, it'll take serious money," Anatoly continued. "Max won't do it at all; it would cost him his job. That means paying a sweetener to his boss or his boss's boss. I can't afford it, unless I get something back."

"Such as?"

"Let me supply Snow Mountain to you again. I've ironed out the quality issues. Thanks to Marina, the business is about to go under. I can turn it around with a single big customer, like you."

"I'd love to help, but I'm about to retire. My company doesn't need supplies from Bazakistan anymore. Kat's Birmingham distillery makes enough to satisfy demand." Marty could imagine what Kat would say if he told her that he was buying vodka from the Aliyev family again.

"I see." Anatoly was clearly angry. "Marina's daughter has you under her spell, as no doubt her mother did before her. It's up to you, my friend. I can't access the financial resources to assist you unless I can be sure the distillery will make money."

What would happen on his retirement without a smooth sale of Darria Enterprises to Jeannie Jenner? He was relying on that cash, and so were his children.

Anyway, Erik's life was at stake. Kat would have to accept the least worst option. Marty was certain he could turn a profit on Anatoly's vodka, too.

He couldn't let Anatoly think there was an open cheque book for him, of course.

"All right. I'll take one consignment to start with. And I want a 10% discount off Marina's old price."

Chapter 27.　　Ben

Ben allowed the prison officer to scan his fingerprint. He hated the rituals of Belmarsh: the long queues, the ID checks, placing valuables in coin lockers and hoping they wouldn't have vanished an hour later. Most of all, he detested the clanging of metal gates locked and unlocked by twitchy guards. By the time he reached the visit hall, he felt as if he was sharing his brother's punishment.

He bought two cups of milky tea and several chocolate bars, keeping his eyes ready for Jon until his brother was brought into the room.

"Here." He passed one drink and all of the food across the Formica table as Jon sat across from him.

"Thanks. Do you remember when we played an all-nighter on the PS2, with only Mars Bars to keep us going?"

"Do I ever." Ben smiled at the thought. "You seem cheerful today."

"Two weeks and I'm out of here."

"Happy days. We'll have a gamesfest to celebrate."

"Got any new ones?" Jon swigged the scalding tea and disposed of a KitKat.

"I'm beta testing a couple." Ben enjoyed this renewed rapport, seemingly sprung from his decision to attend Jon's murder trial in the summer.

Emboldened, he asked Jon, "What else are you planning?"

"I'll open a gym. Maybe start as a personal trainer. I work out every day." Jon rolled back the sleeves of his jumper to reveal strongly muscled arms.

"What about Vince? When does he get out?"

"I don't know. He's not in Belmarsh; they moved him to the coast." Jon seemed curiously unconcerned.

"I thought you shared a cell?"

"Never." Jon sounded bored. "Vince has HIV."

Ben swallowed his instinctive yelp of surprise.

"Don't worry; I haven't." Jon's tone was cold. "I'm not careless. I didn't get off my head on spice, and let the screws find my stash, either."

"Doesn't that mean extra time?"

"And going on basic. Don't bother feeling sorry for him. He's a moron."

Jon sounded hard, but who could blame him, when he'd been forced to grow up so fast? After their mother died, Jon was virtually left to his own devices, until he had to run what remained of the family's criminal empire when their father was imprisoned. Of course he couldn't afford to be sentimental.

"Never mind Vince, anyway. Tell me about the new games."

Along with more tea and chocolate, that filled the rest of the hour. Ben was in a better mood when he departed, although his spirits always lightened as he left the prison car park.

Today, his evening would be special. Amy was visiting his flat for the first time.

Ben reflected on preparations as he drove past the boxy new houses and industrial estates that hugged the south-eastern fringes of the Thames. This was the side of London the tourists never saw: an unlovely, traffic-choked sprawl. The school day was ending, signalling the start of the rush hour. It took ninety minutes to travel home to the more glamorous environs of Fitzrovia.

He parked his Golf GTi and called into the local supermarket for wine. Prosecco was what all the girls liked. He added a couple of tinned cocktails: Cosmopolitans. Ben had no idea what they were, but Amy had let him buy her one before. Flowers would be a nice touch, too. He purchased the first bunch he saw, a bouquet of pink carnations.

Outside, Ben remembered he had nothing in which to display the blooms. He wandered into a homeware shop on Tottenham Court Road, selecting a vase and then deciding a set of crystal glasses would also impress. They were flute-shaped, cut with geometric patterns to catch the light.

There was no need to buy anything else; they could order pizza and ice cream later. He had to throw away the old takeaway cartons littering his flat, however. Hastily, he returned there, filling a bin bag with rubbish before flicking a damp cloth over obvious dust and stains.

Exhausted, he was about to slump on the sofa with his laptop when he realised he'd overlooked the fridge. It contained mouldy food, while a layer of permafrost clung to the inner walls and filled the freezer box. There was nothing he could do about the ice, but the stale food went in the bin. He took the vegetable crisper to the sink and rinsed it, having unearthed a furry mass that was once a strawberry. Finally, he put the fizz in the fridge and settled down with a game.

He was so engrossed, he hardly heard the buzzer announcing Amy's arrival. Despite his joy, he hit the save button before using his phone to admit her to the lobby and tell her to take the lift.

He opened the door, standing across the threshold to wait for her.

To his relief, as she emerged from the lift, he saw another bottle of prosecco in her hand. He'd guessed right about that.

"Great to see you. Let me put that in the fridge." He reached for the wine with one arm, hugging her with the other despite the droplets of water on her sky-blue raincoat.

She kissed his cheek. Feeling a rush of desire, Ben aimed for her lips in reciprocation. He missed, as Amy wriggled out of his grasp and through the doorway.

"Where can I leave my coat?" She looked near the door, her eyes scanning the shiny chrome chain and plethora of bolts fixed to it. "Why the high security?"

"You know how it is in London."

"Even Dee isn't that paranoid."

Ben couldn't admit he'd installed new locks in response to Kyle's warning. Ironically, he didn't need them now he was reconciled with Jon. "Sit down and I'll get you a drink," he said, pointing to the sofa in the centre of the room. It faced away from the door, towards the huge wall-mounted screen he'd hooked up to his state-of-the-art Alienware laptop.

"You're playing a game. Which one?" Amy stared at the frozen tableau of space troopers.

He was about to explain when her phone rang.

Amy fished it out of her handbag. "Oops, it's the boss. I'd better answer that." She swiped upwards.

Ben could tell that the conversation wasn't going well. Her sparkle faded, the colour leaving her already pale face.

"All right, I'm on it," he heard her say, before she tapped the display to end her call.

"What's wrong?"

"That was Marty." She was trembling. "Erik's in jail in Bazakistan. If only he'd asked me before flying over there like that."

Ben inched towards Amy, arms ready to embrace her.

"No, I have to go." Her voice was bleak. "Marty's called a meeting in Birmingham first thing tomorrow morning. I can't stay in London now."

Chapter 28.   Kat

Despite the urgency of the situation, sitting around the oval table in Marty's office felt like a tea party. He poured hot drinks and handed round biscuits while Kat glared at him, impatience vying with suspicion. Whenever Marty acted the kind host, he wanted something.

Tim helped himself to two shortbread fingers and Amy asked for green tea, a zero-calorie option sure to maintain her stick-thin figure. Amy's face was pale and worried, but even so, how could she behave as if this was an everyday marketing meeting? Why was Tim there – did Marty think Kat would be hysterical otherwise?

Marty finished dispensing refreshments. "I'll come straight to the point."

Kat bit her tongue. He could have done it sooner.

"Erik is being held against his will in Bazakistan. I've contacted the Foreign Office." Marty's face wasn't hopeful.

"What are they doing?" Tim asked. He squeezed Kat's hand.

"Too early to say." Marty stirred sugar into his coffee. "Meanwhile, I'm exploring other avenues. Erik is being pressured to move his darria research to Bazakistan. I can't allow it. We'll be doubling up on costs…"

"It's dangerous too. He'd have to base himself there. Erik won't do it, will he?" Kat said hotly, pulling her hand away from Tim's. More and more evidence was showing that Bazakistan wasn't a safe place to do business, at least not if your name was White or Belov. Surely Erik could see that now?

"He's declined so far, but he's been imprisoned for it," Marty said. He must have guessed what she would think, for he added, "It's not your mother's doing. She faces the firing squad."

She deserved it. It was the fate to which Marina had consigned Kat's father. Once, Kat might have shed tears at her mother's death. Now, the news sounded like poetic justice.

Tim, misjudging the bleakness of her true feelings towards Marina, caught Kat's eye. His gaze radiated sympathy. "Dad, we've heard enough. Can Kat and I take some time out, please?"

"Wait." Marty's stern tone jarred against Tim's kindness. "There's a chance that Erik can be rescued, but it has strings attached. I'd have to buy vodka from the Snow Mountain distillery in Kireniat again."

"That's great news," Tim said. "You're working flat out, aren't you, Kat, with Christmas only a month away? That would give us more capacity…"

"Run that past me once more," Kat interjected. "The last time they supplied you, there were lethal quality problems. Every bottle had methanol in it. And how does buying vodka help us get Erik back home?"

"First things first. There was methanol contamination under Marina's ownership," Marty pointed out. "It's not her distillery anymore."

"Who owns it now?" Kat asked.

"Anatoly Aliyev."

Kat glared at Marty. He'd taken leave of his senses. "The old thief's bastard? How can you trust a word he says?"

Marty returned her fierce gaze. "Whatever your feeling towards them, I've never had reason to mistrust either Tolya Aliyev or his father. And Tolya's the only show in town."

"You mentioned the British government – the Foreign Office," Kat said.

Marty shrugged. "I've approached them, but I won't rely on them. Did they rescue you or me, when we were kidnapped by terrorists?"

"We should try everything." Tim's tone remained placatory. "Dad, you were saying?"

Marty continued. "Tolya thinks he can get Erik out of prison and away through the mountains, but he needs money to do it. He'll get it by sending us a consignment. As Tim says, it'll help us satisfy Christmas orders."

"How do you know anyone will buy Bazaki vodka from us? Starshine is our biggest seller these days, and I've been making Snow Mountain here in Birmingham for two years now. I did it as a favour to you, pushing the concept of a UK brand, precisely because of the methanol problem. Can't you just send Anatoly Aliyev the money he wants? You've got plenty of it."

"Please, Kat." Amy's lips were quivering, her eyes wet.

Marty squirmed in his seat. "Here, bab." He fished a travel pack of folded tissues from his pocket, handing one to Amy.

"Thanks." Amy dabbed at the moisture, sniffing. "Look, Kat. We have to make this work. Tim, surely we can develop a marketing concept for vodka from Bazakistan?"

Tim nodded, his empathy obviously focused on Amy. "Of course. We can come up with a totally new brand. The spirit of the mysterious East, perhaps. There's no need to prejudice the Snow Mountain and Starshine trademarks."

Kat gawped at all three of them. Tim and Amy so often failed to agree, but desperation was transforming them into best buddies. Marty was behaving out of character too; he was usually hardnosed, but Anatoly Aliyev was playing him like a puppet on a string.

She sighed. With her brother's life on the line, what choice did any of them have? If only she could guarantee that Aliyev really would save Erik.

Chapter 29.   Erik

Erik thought two nights had elapsed since his world shrank to a small concrete cube. In the grey box, there was no daylight, merely constant illumination from a dim bulb above. Sleep and hunger guided him in the passage of time.

With a clatter and screech, the metal door was unlocked. The rat-faced youth stood at the threshold. "Hello," he said, in heavily-accented English.

"Good morning, Vic, how are you?" Isolated in his cell, Erik had decided to teach English to the guards, when they could be bothered to linger. It would keep madness at bay.

Vic evidently didn't understand the simple phrase. He removed a tin dish of porridge from a steel trolley and gingerly handed the food to Erik.

"Ah, breakfast. Thank you." Erik repeated the words in Russian when there was no reply.

Vic nodded, before locking up again.

A spoon was provided; an improvement on yesterday, when Erik had been forced to drink the sludgy mess straight from the bowl. Ravenous, he ate the disgusting gruel with an emotion approaching relish.

He should mark the wall somehow, otherwise he'd soon forget which day it was. Laboriously, he used the spoon's handle to etch three parallel lines in the rough concrete.

He was alone with his imagination now. Concern for his mother dominated it, punctuated with dark thoughts about Amy. She was always going to meetings in London, staying overnight. It hadn't been necessary when Marty only sold Snow Mountain vodka, so why was it essential for Starshine? She'd had a birthday card last month from someone called Ben; who was he?

Erik suspected Kat had answers, but wasn't saying.

His bleak musings were disturbed by a racket in the corridor.

"No! Leave me alone."

Fear raced through him at the sound of his mother's voice.

The clanking of chains, the thud of footsteps and her screams grew nearer and louder.

His own shackles prevented Erik from getting close to the door. Through the observation slit, he saw her being frogmarched between two guards. "Mother!"

He heard his mother inhale sharply with surprise. She stopped wailing. "Stay strong, my son," she called.

"Don't forget I love you," Erik shouted back.

She disappeared from view in an instant, silent now, as they hurried her along.

After a while, Erik heard the distant sound of gunfire: several sharp and almost simultaneous retorts. Turning his face to the wall, he sobbed, silently, so his captors couldn't gain satisfaction from it. Nevertheless, he waited for his mother to return. He waited a long time. He waited until he'd eaten another bowl of porridge and scratched another line on the wall.

It wasn't Vic who came for Erik, but an older man he hadn't met before. Stocky, balding, face round and flattish, he wasn't inclined to talk.

"What's your name?"

"You're seeing Leo. That's all you need to know. Are you coming quietly, or do we need the chains?"

"I'll behave."

Unshackled and released from his cell, Erik followed the guard through the maze to Dinara's lobby.

The secretary greeted them with a nod, sloe eyes cold. There was no offer of tea. Dinara was wearing emerald green today: another well-fitted dress. Before leaving, his escort ogled her curves. So, Erik noted, did Leo.

Lounging at his desk in the inner sanctum, Leo was smoking a cigarette. He pointed to the packet on his desk.

"Like one?"

"No, thanks. I don't smoke."

Leo shrugged, insolently blowing a cloud in Erik's direction. "Sit." Erik complied.

"You want the LitePro set up?" Dinara asked.

"Yes, please."

She busied herself, unfurling a white screen on a display stand. It occupied most of the wall next to the door, opposite Leo's desk. The position was perfect for Leo's line of vision, while obliging Erik to turn around.

Erik wondered whether Leo had given orders for his mother's fate, or even pulled the trigger. He forced his fists to unclench and his breath to slow.

Dinara fetched a black box roughly the same size and shape as a bag of flour. When placed on Leo's desk and connected with a lead to his laptop, this turned out to be a projector. Eric, used to Marty's expensive corporate toys, thought it quaint.

"You may leave, Dinara." Leo stubbed out the cigarette with one hand, clicking his mouse with the other.

Grainy black and white footage filled the screen: six policemen with rifles aiming at a petite blonde woman in dark sweatshirt and jeans. The guns recoiled and the woman jerked backwards, falling to the ground.

"You see what happens to enemies of the state?" Anger blazed in Leo's brown eyes.

Erik sat, still and stony-faced. He was done with tears. Leo wouldn't see any.

Leo stood up, pacing around his desk. Emanating menace, he loomed over Erik. "The state has a moral right to your darria patent. Transfer it to us."

"I've told you, I can't." Erik kept his voice calm. "It belongs to Darria Enterprises and I only have half of the shares."

"Then transfer your shares to us. This is the last time I'll ask nicely."

"No."

Leo slapped his face, a signet ring stinging Erik's cheek and drawing blood. "Crazy man. You want to die?"

Erik met his angry gaze with silence.

He owed nothing to the state of Bazakistan, except revenge. It had taken away his parents and cast his sister into exile. Kat hated the Bazaki government even more than he did, so she'd understand. Amy didn't want him anymore. His research would survive him, because Marty, keen to make money, would engage the best scientists to make sure it did.

Erik reached his decision. It wasn't difficult.

"Some things are worth dying for," he said.

127

Chapter 30.   Marty

To Marty's relief, the offer from Jenner Investments hadn't been withdrawn – at any rate, not yet. He was wary as he emerged from Old Street Tube station, however. Charles's emailed request for a meeting hadn't mentioned Erik, but it was inconceivable that the investors didn't know what was happening.

This part of London reminded Marty of the crumbling, less gentrified fringes of Birmingham's Jewellery Quarter. As well as chichi media studios and zen cocktail bars, he noted dubious phone shops and graffiti. It seemed an odd location for the nerve centre of Jeannie Jenner's business empire.

His destination was on Shoreditch High Street in an old factory building. It was a red brick cuboid adorned with a grid of windows, titivated and repurposed. The capital's treatment of its industrial heritage wasn't very different from Birmingham's. Marty almost felt at home, especially as the six-storey reception lobby didn't boast the potted trees and fountains he expected from swish London offices. Instead, he was greeted by bare breeze block walls, exposed pipes and a grey lino floor. A bicycle rack held pricy-looking machines. In front of this was a cabin of the sort occupied by watchmen on building sites.

Its occupant, a dreadlocked white man in hoodie and jeans, scrutinised Marty. "Can I help you?"

"Are you the receptionist?"

"Sure. Who you are looking for?"

"I'm seeing Charles Satterthwaite and Davey Saxton at Jenner Investments."

"Level four." He jerked a tanned thumb at two lift cages, rope wires visible as they moved up and down one side of the space. As an apparent afterthought, he added, "You'd better have one of these," and handed over an orange lanyard with a badge that proclaimed 'Visitor'.

There was a lift waiting when Marty pressed for it. It rattled its way to the fourth floor, persuading him he should find the stairs for his return to the ground later. When it disgorged him, he saw the words 'Jenner Investments' etched onto a glass door to the left, with a buzzer next to it.

"Any news on Erik?" Charles opened the door, his casual blue jumper and cream chinos at odds with his taut stance.

"Stalemate. Still in jail. He's been told to sign his shares over to the Bazaki nation, and he's refused." Marty shook his head. "I don't know how reliable the tidings are. They're third-hand, via a bribed secretary."

Charles winced, ushering him inside. The old factory was now a light, white open-plan workplace for industrious-looking young people tapping at laptops. Some sat at desks, others on primary-coloured beanbags. A few clustered in glass-walled rooms, dotted around at random like giant sugar cubes.

"Where's your office?" Marty asked.

"I don't have one." Charles pointed to a glass cubicle in which a man sat at a small plywood table. "There's Davey."

Tall and informally dressed like Charles, Davey stood as they entered, making Marty feel short and overly fussy in suit and tie. At least Davey had even less hair than he did.

"Have you met Davey?" Charles asked. "He was at my wedding party last year."

That had been the wedding that didn't take place. "I recognise you, but we weren't introduced then," Marty said. "You're Charles's brother-in-law, aren't you?"

Davey grinned. "Yes, Dee's brother. I admit she's prettier than me, before you make any comment. Charles and I go back years, too. He's been my schoolfriend, team-mate and IT director." Well-spoken, a slight twang hinted at origins near London.

"Now I'm working for him again. I can't keep away," Charles remarked. Taking a cue from Davey, he seemed more at ease.

"Totally lacking in common sense. Why do I employ him?" Davey said. "Anyway, Marty I've just joined Jenner Investments as CEO, and I've made changes already. Including moving the head office here so we can attract the right kind of staff, present company excepted."

"Not because Davey lives next door," Charles said.

"Or because Charles can cycle in via the Regent's Canal," Davey retorted.

"Which, as you ask, has a towpath."

"Thanks for inviting me here," Marty said.

"You're too polite, Marty. The word is 'summoned'." Davey smiled, signalling it was a joke. "Sit down, and Charles will get you a coffee. I ask him simply because he's a devil with the espresso machine."

The unprepossessing meeting chairs, made of a web of white plastic, were surprisingly comfortable. Marty lounged back. It didn't relax him. He liked to have more control of a meeting. "I assume you've got questions about financials," he asked.

"If they're different from what Guy sent me."

Charles returned with two red mugs apparently filled with white foam. "Hope this merits the Bridges seal of approval, Marty," he said. "I'll leave you with Davey, but if you want a pint later, let me know."

A rich aroma of coffee filled the cubicle.

"So," Davey said when Charles had closed the glass door behind him, "we are planning a significant investment in your cancer-busting drug, and it seemed a good idea to meet. We'd like to know more about you, and you'll want to know about us. I'll kick off, shall I?"

Marty sipped his latte. It was pleasingly strong. "Fine."

"Good plan, eh? I'm sure Guy's told you that this company is Jeannie Jenner's personal investment vehicle. It owns the bedrock of her wealth, an engineering conglomerate that makes many of the electrical goods you'll find in your household: washing machines, kitchen equipment and so on. Also computer chips, which is the big earner. We are putting those profits into a diversified portfolio of investments, with an ethical angle. I should ask, do you read the tabloids?"

"My wife takes the Daily Mail."

"Mine did too. I mean, presumably she still does, but she's no longer my wife." Davey didn't seem upset about it. "Jeannie is my partner, as you'd undoubtedly be aware should you happen to scan the gossip columns."

"Amy mentioned it." Marty didn't need to read rumour mills.

"I didn't get this job because of my relationship, however, but thanks to my experience. I've run two insurance companies."

"I know," Marty told him. "I had kidnap insurance with one of them." To Angela's devastation, no cash had been forthcoming from Saxton Brown when he'd been kidnapped in Bazakistan. He hadn't bothered renewing the policy after his escape.

Davey remembered it differently. "Your breakout was brilliant," he enthused. "It saved us loads of money. As I was saying, apart from niche policies like yours, there was a major investment component in my work. When Jeannie's last CEO suddenly resigned six months ago, she asked me to step in." He added, "She's very interested in your research. A good friend of hers has cancer and the prognosis is dire. I don't suppose any of that darria drug could find its way to them, could it?"

"What you do once you own the business is up to you." Marty recalled Erik explaining circumstances in which individuals could access drugs at the trial stage. He wished he'd listened more carefully; there might have been an opportunity to earn money from it.

"So, in a nutshell, that's us. Any questions?"

"Just one," Marty said, edging towards the elephant in the room. "If, say, there was a move to run extra clinical trials in Bazakistan, the birthplace of the darria herb, how would you feel about it?"

Davey fingered his chin, reflecting. "I know why you're asking. The Bazaki government has its hooks in Erik White. They want the intellectual property in the drug and they're using him as leverage."

They did have the whole story, then, as Marty had expected. "I'm trying to get Erik out," he said.

"So am I," Davey replied, to Marty's surprise.

"What are you going to do?"

"I called the business attaché at the British embassy in Bazaku City," Davey said. "He explained the local political landscape: the balancing act between nationalist politicians, big business and the military. They all hate, but depend on, each other. Corporations, especially foreign ones, are seen as too powerful. It would play out well with the public if your cancer drug was nationalised – brought back to Bazakistan, as it were."

"Why would anyone care?" Marty asked, flabbergasted. "They don't have free elections in Bazakistan, anyhow. Everyone knows that."

Davey raised an eyebrow. "The President has to keep his populace happy. If there's a riot, it's an excuse for the army to step in. In the blink of an eye, the country's under military rule. Still, you asked what I was going to do?"

Marty stared at him. Davey's body language betrayed nothing.

"The drug has value without Erik's guiding hand. You've worked that out, Marty, I'm sure. We can buy in scientific expertise, but it will add research time and costs, while the patent's expiry date stays fixed. The window for commercialisation will be shorter."

Marty could see it coming: Davey would drop the price.

"More fundamental, though, it's personal for Jeannie. Her friend can't wait. Jeannie wants Erik back here and she's prepared to spend a bit of money, perhaps endow a chair at one of the top universities in Bazakistan."

Davey placed his hands on the table, palms up. There was a shrewd glimmer in his eyes. "I've told my attaché friend to negotiate."

Chapter 31.   Erik

Erik had the haziest notion it might be Thursday. He counted the lines on the wall: fifteen. He was right. It was a small victory.

The second of the day's two meals, a thin vegetable soup and flatbread, had been served and cleared away. As usual, Erik was still hungry. Already slim, he felt his clothes hanging loose, the angles of his ribs and pelvic bones becoming more prominent.

He heard footsteps in the corridor: Vic, the rat-faced guard, his ablest student.

"Hello, how are you?" Vic's English was still slow, but much easier to understand. "Good news." A key jangled in the lock, and the door clanked open.

Erik shielded his eyes as brighter light from the passage spilled into the cell. "Good afternoon. I'm fine, thank you," he said. It was a lie. His mother's death and his abandonment in this cell were eating his soul. "How is the weather outside?"

"It's evening, and it's snowing." Vic switched to Russian. He thrust a bundle of clothes at Erik. "Here. Put these on quickly, or you'll miss the last flight."

"What do you mean? The last flight where?" Erik matched him in Russian.

"London."

Erik stared at him in disbelief.

"It's true. Hurry up."

"Why now?" For a fortnight, no one had visited except the guards. There had been no communication from family, friends, colleagues or officials. As far as he knew, they'd forgotten about him.

"Who can say? It's above my pay grade. I've been told you're going home, that's all."

"Aren't you forgetting something?" He pointed to the shackles on his legs. A chain secured them to a metal ring on the wall, ensuring he couldn't reach the doorway or anyone standing at the threshold.

"Of course." Vic applied a key to the ankle cuffs. "Sorry, I have to watch while you change. Orders."

"I won't try to escape."

Vic's response was a grin, but he averted his eyes.

Erik unpeeled the sticky, sweaty garments he'd worn for two weeks. He recognised the fresh outfit, neat and pressed, as a selection of items from his suitcase. The aroma of washing powder smelled precious as any perfume; the clean cotton against his skin felt sybaritic. He would have liked to brush his teeth, shave and shower too. Perhaps he could do that at the airport. He allowed hope to rise.

A worm of doubt began to gnaw at his excitement. What if Vic was lying? This could be a trap. Even if it wasn't, no airline would allow him to fly without a passport. He'd seen it crumple and burn to ashes under the flame of Leo's lighter.

"We'll go to Leo now," Vic said, increasing Erik's misgivings.

Comfort came from a subtle change in Vic's attitude. The officer was almost deferential. They walked side by side, Vic insisting on a final opportunity to practise English curses.

The route to Leo's office seemed even more complicated than before. Like London cab drivers learning the Knowledge, the policemen who worked here must have to memorise a map of the whole building. Vic had impressed on him the need for speed, yet they were wasting time negotiating this warren.

"When does the plane leave?" Erik asked.

"Don't worry. Leo will make sure you're there."

They arrived at the oak door. Vic rapped smartly upon it.

"He's waiting." Dinara, in a red dress and heels, was dolled up for a night out. She must be working late. Her snub nose wrinkled as she ushered Erik into her cubbyhole. Away from the overpowering tang of disinfectant, he was aware that he reeked of sweat. It was too bad if the smell lingered in her office afterwards; she could blame her boss.

Leo wasn't lounging with his feet on the desk this time. He sat upright, apparently in conversation with a man sitting opposite, a professional-looking type in a suit, with short ginger hair. Both stood as Erik walked into the room.

"Jake Reever from the British embassy." The man extended his hand. He was fresh-faced, possibly not yet thirty, with an impeccable English public school accent.

"Erik White. Am I really being released?" Erik shook Reever's hand, being rewarded with a bone-crushing grip from Leo as well.

Rather than answer, Reever turned to Leo. "Are you sure this is the right man? There's no beard in any of the photographs I've seen."

"Would you like to shave, Mr White? We can arrange that." Leo's command of English, his use of Erik's surname and ability to be polite were faultless when he made an effort.

"I would, yes please."

Dinara was summoned and told to organise it. Five minutes later, she returned with a Gillette razor and a stick of deodorant.

"Take him to the men's washroom," Leo ordered.

She complied, scowling as soon as she was out of her boss's sight. "I'll wait outside," she told Erik. "There should be soap and towels. See me if there aren't."

The white-tiled basin inside was, at least, clean. A small mirror hung above, and a greying hand towel next to it. Erik knew removing a fortnight's growth would hurt, especially without foam or gel. He lathered the single bar of soap as best he could, spreading the creamy suds over his face.

The multi-blade razor caught and tugged his unwanted hairs, exceeding Erik's expectations of pain. Finally, a smooth chin emerged. Aware of his odour, he stripped and soaped his hair and body, rinsing and towelling himself before applying deodorant. The sensation of cleanliness was exquisite.

Reever nodded on his return, evidently satisfied of his identity. "So," the diplomat said, "I gather your passport was lost and you ended up in police custody as a result?"

"No," Erik began.

Leo interrupted him. "I regret that your detention lasted for such a long period. We normally don't keep anyone in our police cells for long. I acknowledge that mistakes were made."

"And, no doubt, lessons learned," Reever said, drily. "Thank you, Mr Denisov. You have Mr White's suitcase, I believe?"

"It's here. Mr Aliyev brought it today." Leo pointed to a black Samsonite cabin case standing by the door.

"Recognise it?" Reever asked.

"Yes." It certainly looked like the one Erik had left with Anatoly. He would have used his own shaving kit if he'd known.

"Good. Here are some temporary travel documents, and an air ticket." Reever handed Erik a clear plastic document wallet containing a few papers. "This will get you home. You can apply for a new passport then."

"You'll need these too." Leo gave Erik his wallet and phone, then looked at his watch. "You'd better leave for the airport. One of our cars will take you."

"An embassy car's waiting," Reever objected.

"It has to be ours, for the traffic."

Leo's explanation sounded implausible, but Reever acquiesced.

"All right. I'll keep Mr White company," the diplomat volunteered.

There was another robust handshake from Leo before he detailed Dinara to escort his guests to their driver.

"Going somewhere nice?" Reever asked her, in perfect Russian.

"The cinema. In ten minutes."

"What are you seeing?"

She began to speak freely as he beguiled her, giving them her life story in the three-minute walk to the station entrance and their waiting driver.

"Goodbye, Dinara. It's been lovely meeting you," Reever said, kissing her cheeks as snow swirled around them. Erik saw that winter had taken hold during his captivity, cloaking unsalted ground with a white layer six inches thick.

Shivering in the frosty air, Erik guessed the diplomat anticipated a future reunion. It didn't hurt to have friends in the police force.

"We'll sit in the back of the car," Reever told the driver. "Erik, you'll be wanting to keep your case with you."

The stripy vehicle was roomy, and the small cabin bag fitted easily onto the seat between them.

Erik relaxed on the soft upholstery. The leatherette was infinitely more comfortable than the concrete bench that had served as bed and sofa in his cell. "I didn't lose my passport," he said.

"You can tell me later," Reever said. "My goodness, look at this weather. I hope Dinara isn't walking to her date. Should get better after Christmas, shouldn't it?"

"Snow in May is not unknown," Erik said. It was only later, in the departure hall at Kireniat airport, that he realised Reever had steered their discussion entirely towards neutral subjects during the thirty-minute journey.

"I know you didn't lose your passport," Reever announced, as they negotiated their way through swing doors into the terminal. "I choose my battles, that's all."

"He burned it."

"I thought as much," Reever said. "Not to worry; they'll let you board. I'll make sure of it. Let's get you checked in."

The diplomatic badge and smooth talking worked wonders at the check-in desk. Erik received a complimentary upgrade to business class.

"I'd go straight through security now, if I were you, rather than hang around," Reever counselled, somewhat unnecessarily in Eric's opinion. "Three things. Your business partner knows you're on this flight, and he's waiting at Heathrow. Second, before they do the security checks, inspect your baggage to confirm the contents are what you expect them to be. Last but not least, when you're home, you'll receive a feedback form. I know it's tedious, but my boss likes our service users to have their say, so please reply. Preferably in the most glowing terms possible."

"No problem," Erik said. "I'm very grateful for your help. You must have been doing a lot for me behind the scenes."

"It's my job."

"What happened, exactly?"

"Unofficially, your business partner oiled the wheels. Bazaku City University will get some money and a mention in research papers. One of the conditions is that you'll never have to go there."

"Thanks." It could be worse. They had killed his mother, but they wouldn't have another chance at him. "I wonder if I could trouble you for a favour? My phone isn't charged. May I borrow yours to call my sister and my girlfriend, please? I won't talk for long – just let them hear my voice and know I'm safe."

Reever agreed, doubtless eager to guarantee fulsome feedback. He pressed a finger to the screen, and handed the phone to Erik.

He tried Amy first. There was no answer. Erik left a message, speculating that Amy and Kat might be out at a Christmas party. He didn't imagine that Kat would take his call now, but in fact, she replied after the first ring.

"Kat, it's Erik. I'm coming home."

"Where are you? This is marvellous." She gushed so much that Erik could see Reever looking impatient.

"I'm landing at Heathrow tomorrow morning. Marty's collecting me. Do you know why Amy's not answering her phone?"

"No idea." Kat's tone hinted that she had an inkling, but wasn't about to share it.

The chill that descended couldn't dispel the exhilaration of freedom. Erik gave the mobile back to Reever. "Thanks," he said, shaking the diplomat's hand. "It's a late night for you."

"They often are. Sometimes, it might even be a drinks party." Reever swung an arm around Erik's shoulder. "It's been a pleasure, Erik. Charge that phone in the lounge, and have a glass of wine. Sleep well on the plane. In the nicest possible way, I hope I never see you again."

Erik watched the diplomat weave through the milling passengers and out into the snow. He walked to the line of travellers waiting by the X-ray machines, about to join them when he recalled Reever's advice to check the contents of his case. It had to be opened, anyway; his laptop and liquids would be carried through the X-ray machine on a separate tray.

He unzipped the bag. The laptop in its black sleeve wasn't resting on top of the folded garments. Someone must have moved it to find him a change of clothes. Erik fumbled through the contents, dismay mounting. His laptop wasn't there.

All his data was backed up, of course, but he'd just made a present of it to the hackers of Bazakistan. They would think Christmas had come three weeks early. What was he going to tell Marty?

Chapter 32.   Ben

"Thanks for offering me a meal, Ben. You're a true friend." Evading a kiss again, Amy slung her handbag on the key table beside his front door, hanging her coat on the hook newly installed nearby.

She was wearing a short navy jumper dress, black tights and long boots. They displayed her slim legs perfectly. A hint of floral scent clung to her.

"Busy day?" He only knew she'd been doing whatever marketing managers did in London. It involved vodka, which should be fun, but she looked tired and drawn. She seemed stone-cold sober, too. He'd better address that. Gesturing towards the sofa, he eased his way left of the door, to the kitchenette corner.

Amy followed him rather than sitting down. "I like your place. I didn't really explore it before."

Ben laughed. "There's not much to see. It's only a studio flat. My bed and shower room are over there, behind the partition." It was almost a wall of cupboards, to the right of the doorway. In a valiant effort to tidy up, he'd flung his belongings into them just before she arrived.

"And you have a view." She followed him to the jet-black granite and high gloss kitchen units, stepping beyond to the stylish table and chairs in front of the balcony. Outside, ornate Victorian streetlamps illuminated a brick and stucco terrace.

"I like it. It's near the bars, but this lane is quiet." He glanced anxiously at the flower vase on the table, suddenly recalling that these were the pink carnations he'd bought two weeks before. Luckily, they were passable: only slightly browned at the edges.

He opened the fridge.

"Ben? All you've got in there is pizza and prosecco."

"All we need, surely? It's Christmas pizza, with turkey and stuffing." Ben grinned to cover his embarrassment.

Amy appeared unimpressed. She inspected the fridge's grubby shelves, opening the takeaway box, then seemed to make up her mind. "That's not a meal. You've had half of it already." She wrinkled her nose. "Pour me a glass of that prosecco, please, if it isn't a health hazard. I'll go to the supermarket on Goodge Street, and buy proper food. Let me cook for you."

Ben wasn't planning to argue. When she flushed like that, she looked even more appealing. He retrieved the bottle and took a pair of crystal flutes from the box that still sat, unopened, on the granite work surface. Luckily, he was sufficiently practised with champagne corks to open the fizz without spilling it.

"Cheers." Comfortable on the sofa next to him, Amy clinked glasses, then drained most of hers. "I so needed this."

"Have another, and tell me what's up." He topped up her prosecco.

She looked at him, despair pulling at the corners of her mouth. "I'm so worried about Erik. He's been in that terrible place for a fortnight, and we've heard barely a word about him. Marty's doing his best, but..." The sentence tailed away. Her gorgeous blue eyes spoke of hopelessness.

"You need more bubbly, and a hug." He refilled her glass. Snuggling into her, he put an arm around her shoulder. Her perfume intoxicated him. The evening was alive with promise.

Glass in hand, she leaned back and relaxed as he stroked her hair.

"You're so good for me," he murmured, gliding his free hand down to brush her thigh.

Amy shook herself from his grip, finished her drink and set the glass on the table. "I'll pop out now for some bits and pieces. More wine too. Lend me your keys, and I'll let myself back in."

Ben saw her to the door, then went to reseal the pizza box. He'd have the contents tomorrow for lunch: not breakfast, because he wanted Amy to stay, and she'd demand something better. A pang of anxiety swept through him. This was beginning to feel like a real date, but was she really into him? He wasn't used to trying so hard: his female fans usually threw themselves at him, especially in the hedonistic aftermath of a tournament.

He decided to calm his jitters by switching on the new Alienware laptop. The mean machine was merely a month old, his pride and joy, bristling with extras. Soon, he'd escaped into Star Legends, the virtual universe of which he was master. His soundbar resonated with thuds and screams as his enemies were vanquished.

He had completely lost track of time when he heard the flip of the lock, and laboured breathing as the door opened. Poor Amy: the lift must have stopped working again, leaving her to carry shopping up two flights of stairs. "Put them down and have some wine," he called, without looking around.

"Where's my glass, bro?" a deep voice drawled.

Ben jolted to his feet, turning to look into his brother's eyes, wide like a cat's. The enlarged pupils betrayed a recent hit, probably of cocaine.

"Yes, I'm home, bro. I'm sorry I didn't write, but I know you love surprises, Benny boy." A kitbag swinging from his shoulder, Jon strutted inside and slammed the door. Ben recognised the designer jeans, grey hoodie and ironic black Hanged Man T-shirt: Jon's favourite clothes from his pre-Belmarsh days.

"Who are you trying to keep out?" Jon examined the bolts and chains. "You've got high security, but it's not good enough. I've had time to sharpen my skills. Lots of time."

He didn't wait for an answer, but swaggered to the kitchenette, picking up the half-empty bottle. "Mind if I help myself?"

"Be my guest. There are four glasses in that box." Ben finally found his voice in this surreal situation.

"Very tidy in here for my sloppy brother. Expecting company?"

"Always," Ben said, trying to appear calm. "Another round of beta-testing. There's a whole team coming around to discuss strategy." He hoped that sounded boring enough to persuade Jon to leave. Otherwise, there would be no cosy night on the sofa with Amy.

"A team? Including the little tart who just went shopping for you?"

Ben stared at him. How did he know?

"Observation. The key to a successful crime. That's what the old man used to say, wasn't it?" Jon laughed. He splashed prosecco into a glass, knocking it back in one. "Lovely bubbly. Shame I'm not going to able to join the party. Shame Dad can't, either. He loved a party."

He let go of the empty flute. It fell, tinkling as it shattered on the laminated wood floor.

"Oops," Jon said. He took another from the box, licked a finger and ran it around the rim to produce a high-pitched tone. "Hear that ringing? The sound of quality crystal. You'd be surprised what Dad taught me."

He dropped that too, cupping his ear for the chimes as it broke. "Nice place you've got here. Nice things. Sorry I'm so clumsy." Jon waved a hand.

Ben noticed, for the first time, that his brother was wearing purple surgical gloves. He opened his mouth to ask why, but his now racing mind answered with sickening clarity before he spoke.

"Look at me, Jon." He tried to make eye contact with his brother. If Jon lost his temper, there would be no reasoning with him. Ben needed to convince him there was an alternative.

Jon's attention turned from his inspection and slow destruction of Ben's breakable possessions. His black-lashed, almost childlike, eyes regarded Ben coldly. "Got something to say, bro?"

"I'm sorry about Dad. You know I had no choice."

"There's always a choice. But you didn't care about Dad, and you don't care about me. You've got all your new, special, friends."

Jon had completed his circuit of the space by now. He swigged the dregs of the prosecco, then hurled the bottle against the toughened glass of the balcony door. This time, the crunch of smashing glass was much louder. "Don't worry, bro. No one's going to hear. Soundly built, these prestige developments."

Ben knew Jon was right. There was never a peep from his neighbours; they didn't complain about the raucous soundtrack to his computer games.

Jon reached into his kitbag, retrieving a white plastic apron. It was the jokey sort they might once have given their mother for Christmas, adorned with a pointing finger and the slogan 'I'm with this idiot'. He looped the ties around his head and waist.

Ben needed no further confirmation of Jon's intentions. He began to inch away from his brother, towards the dining table and chairs. He'd slip out onto the balcony and raise the alarm. He shuddered, wondering if anyone would hear his cries for help before he was forced to jump. Some people survived higher falls than that.

Jon's gaze fixed on a knife block with six stainless steel handles protruding from it. Like most of his kitchen equipment, Ben had bought it in the expectation of learning to cook, before deciding it was too much trouble.

Jon removed the longest blade, a bread knife. He held it before him like a sword, examining it, then dropped it into his kitbag. One by one, he did the same with the others, until only the sharpest and smallest remained, the paring knife. He pulled it out slowly, then rolled back a sleeve and lightly scored a cross on his own forearm with the tip. "Perfect," he whispered.

Ben nudged the dining chair in front of the window.

"You'll never jump. You're a coward, Ben. We both know that." Jon sprang towards Ben, blocking his escape, flourishing the knife. "We can do this the hard way – or the other way."

As a cold sweat enveloped him, Ben smelled his own fear. He felt sure Jon could sense it too. "Do what?" He tried to sound strong and invincible, like an older brother should.

Jon's face was close, his breath a mix of alcohol and skunk. "In my bag, I have a rope and a shiny silver roll of gaffer tape. You can sit down and listen. Or, we'll have a fight, and you'll lose. Then you'll sit down and listen."

Ben sat down heavily. The flimsy plywood and chrome chair flexed under him. He heard his own panicked breathing. "Why?" he asked, his throat and fingers clenched.

Jon sat opposite, elbows on the table, blade on display. "It's a family thing," he rasped.

"We're family, Jon. You're all I have." Ben peered at his brother. It was hard to believe that this wild-eyed man was the chatty little boy Ben remembered from childhood, or the rueful reformed sinner hopeful of parole, welcoming letters and prison visits.

"Am I really?" Jon's face exuded contempt. "I don't think so. You were always different, thinking you were too good for us. University, jet-setting with your gaming friends." Spittle flecked his lips. "Dad said let it ride. Not anymore. You shot him. As soon as you killed him, you should have known I'd come for you."

"You told Clive to back off."

"Right. Because it's between you and me."

"It was him or me, Jon. Can't you see that? Only one of us could get out of that room alive."

"It should have been him. He should have walked out of there, just like I'll walk out of here." Jon was shouting. Tears spilled from his bloodshot eyes.

"I only ever wanted to help him, to stop him killing somebody."

"He didn't need your sort of help. And neither do I." Jon spat the words, his rage thickening. "I'm fitter and harder than you can imagine."

Ben pushed against the back of his chair, as Jon lifted the blade of the knife to rest on his throat.

"You're scared now, aren't you, Benny boy? Not the clever one now."

"You don't want to do this, Jon. They'll catch up with you, and then you'll end up…"

"Do you think I care? Have you been listening? Do you ever listen? Dad was my world, my hero, and you took him away." Blinking the tears from his eyes, Jon sat back and slammed the knife into the table.

Could he reach the front door? Ben took his chance. He swept an arm at the flower vase, shoving it into Jon's chest before jumping to his feet and into the gap between sofa and coffee table.

The stomping sound of Jon's Doc Martens was proof of his instant reactions. Without stopping to consider his affection for the Alienware laptop, Ben picked it up, turned and threw the heavy object at his brother.

Jon stumbled momentarily, leaping upwards again like a coiled spring.

It bought Ben time to make it to the other end of the sofa and lunge behind it. He reached for the door handle. As he grasped it, his brother's hands were on him, pulling him by the hair and clothes down to the floor. Struggling made no difference. Jon's muscled arm hooked him around until Ben was flat on his back, his head squashed against the rear of the sofa, with Jon straddled across his torso.

"Now we'll talk. Oh, yes." Jon pressed the knife to Ben's throat again, harder, piercing the skin.

Ben gagged at the biting pain and metallic odour.

"A pinprick," Jon said, scornfully. He slashed a cheek, the shallow cut sending blood trickling into Ben's mouth, nose and eyes. "That was for me. The next one's for Dad."

Ben struggled uselessly under his brother's weight, screaming as Jon hacked at an ear, knowing he had no other audience. "I'm sorry," he gasped, retching as bile caught his throat.

"Too little, too late," Jon sneered. "Let's have another for Dad." He played with the knife, drumming the handle on Ben's chest and dancing the blade along one upper arm, chest and across to the other arm before plunging it into the flesh below the shoulder socket. Removing the weapon, he wriggled the sharp point through the weft of Ben's T-shirt, teasing his ribs.

Hair and clothes sticky with blood, pain overwhelming him, Ben's consciousness drifted.

He didn't see what happened next, just heard the door open, followed by a crunching noise as Jon slumped forward onto his face and chest.

There was a hiss of gas escaping, the smell of wine, and more thuds as Jon's body pressed down even harder on his.

Ben began to choke, unable to breathe. Then, as if it had wings, the heavy load was lifted from him and Amy was screaming his name.

Chapter 33.   Marty

Fortified by strong coffee and a rubbery egg and bacon bap, Marty waited in the arrivals lounge at Heathrow. There was a chill wind outside, and sleet had lashed his Jag as he headed south on the M40. He was glad of the warm air within.

Around him, families were hugging each other. Bleary-eyed businessmen were nodding to curt chauffeurs. Marty scanned the stream of passengers emerging landside, irritated at the thought of his bill for short stay parking. Erik's plane had landed an hour ago. Unfortunately, it seemed several others had too. The lines at the passport gates must be horrendous.

Eventually, he spotted Erik, pulling a small wheeled case. His business partner looked haggard, his eyes reddened and unfocused. Marty waved.

Erik headed towards him. "Marty, thank you for getting me out of that hellhole. I thought I'd die in the grey box, like my mother."

"Marina's dead? I'm sorry to hear it." Marty tried to sound sincere for Erik's sake. He had no sympathy for Marina Aliyeva.

"Can you drive me into London? I want to see Amy right now."

"Can't you wait until tonight? The bab should finish her meetings in the Smoke today."

While the M40 wouldn't be fun in the rush hour, a drive into central London was worse. Still, Erik's eagerness to be with Amy proved there was nothing amiss with their relationship. That was a relief; she'd help him recover from his ordeal.

"I phoned her when I landed. She told me she'd spent all night in hospital." Erik's eyes showed his distress.

"Really? What's up?"

"Amy didn't say much. She was trying to break up a fight, apparently."

"Happens in the best of pubs, I suppose. Is she all right?"

"She's not injured, but she's had a shock. I want to be with her."

"Of course." Marty was philosophical now he understood the circumstances. This was more than a lover's whim. "Find the hospital's postcode, and we'll drive straight there."

He led Erik to the car park, seeking a pay station, unsurprised by the hefty charge when he found one. A full day's parking in Birmingham would be cheaper. Thanks to Amy's predicament, he'd also be penalised with a congestion charge for daring to bring the Jag into central London. Birmingham City Council was considering a similar levy. As if he didn't pay enough tax already, the government continually conspired to find novel ways to increase the burden.

Resentment threatened to engulf him. Marty decided the best way to improve his mood was to quiz Erik about his privations. He thrust the case in the boot of his car, and gestured to Erik to take the passenger seat.

"You've lost weight," he said.

"Prison food. What there is, you have to eat before the cockroaches get it. It's no holiday camp."

"Want to tell me about it?"

"In a minute. I've got that postcode for you, Marty. It's University College Hospital, NW1 2BU."

Marty punched in details, then joined the queue for the car park exit.

"About your laptop," he said to Erik.

His business partner looked stricken. "I'm very sorry, Marty. How did you know I'd lost it?"

"You haven't." Marty laughed at the bewilderment on Erik's face. "As soon as you were banged up, I asked Tolya Aliyev to send it to me. He retrieved it from your suitcase and had it airfreighted by courier."

"Thank goodness. I was afraid all our secrets had been hacked."

"Yes, like my bank account." That still rankled.

"Tolya's been helpful, then?" Erik said. "He seemed pleasant, but in jail, I had cause to question my trust in him. I can't be sure he wasn't involved either in my imprisonment or my mother's."

"I don't know about her," Marty said, suspecting the best case was that Anatoly hadn't lifted a finger, "but for you, he made an effort. He tried to bribe politicians, and have you smuggled you out of the country."

"Instead, diplomacy did the trick. With a push from you."

Marty, swinging the Jag onto the road, risked a sharp sideways glance. "A bung from Jenner Investments. Davey Saxton did a deal with Bazaku City University. It all comes down to money, even with Tolya. He's keen to sell me vodka."

"Will you buy it?"

"That's up to Kat," Marty said. "She didn't like Tolya's father. In my view, Tolya himself was more sinned against, than sinning. Certainly, so far as your mother was concerned."

147

"She went to the firing squad," Erik said, seconds before Marty turned right to join the M4 towards London.

Marty squinted at the morning sun shining low on the eastern horizon. It wouldn't be tactful to remind Erik his father had died the same way, thanks to Marina.

"I saw her just before it happened," Erik said. He fell silent.

"Don't torture yourself. You went above and beyond for her. You put your own life at risk."

"It didn't do any good, just caused you a heap of trouble."

"That's over now. Try to move on. Why not snatch some sleep, so you're fresh when you see Amy? I'll concentrate on the road. It's like Brum traffic on steroids."

Erik closed his eyes. He was quiet, his expression careworn. A deep slumber would have erased the tense lines on his face, so if he dozed at all, he did so fitfully.

The M4 dissolved into a local highway, redlined at the roadside and still busy with pulsing traffic. They were in the urban sprawl of Chiswick, miles yet from London's centre. Passing the Fuller's brewery, Marty yearned briefly for a pint. He was desperate for more caffeine too, having been up at five.

Erik's phone rang. Marty's business partner jolted upright. "Yes, Amy?" There was a brief discussion, then Erik said, "All right. Primrose Hill."

Marty waited for Erik to finish. "Let me guess. Charles has picked her up."

"You're right."

"Good." They stopped at a red signal. Marty hastily reprogrammed the satnav, telling it to avoid the congestion charge zone.

Driving rain began whipping the windscreen as the Jag wiggled through backstreets north of Regent's Park. The gracious houses and skeletal winter trees reminded Marty of Edgbaston. Charles's property, a white stucco semi with trophy cars on the drive, was like a smaller version of his own mansion. It was undoubtedly worth much more: everything in London was overpriced.

The on-road spaces were for residents only. Marty swivelled his Jag onto the foot of the drive, boxing in Dee's customised red Mini and Charles's yellow Porsche 911 Turbo. "Don't fret about Amy," he said to Erik, "she'll cheer up the minute she sets eyes on you."

He rang the doorbell, a ceramic button set in a brass circle. It had probably summoned servants a hundred years ago. Today, Charles answered it.

"Thank goodness you're back." Charles clapped a hand on Erik's shoulder. "Come in. Amy's catching up on her zeds in the spare bedroom."

"I need to see her. Is she all right?" Erik, overtired and edgy, was obviously running on adrenaline.

"She's okay, but I'd give her a chance to rest, if I were you. She's only been in bed for an hour."

"What exactly happened?"

"She stopped two men from killing each other. I don't know much more, but don't worry; there's not a scratch on her." Charles regarded Erik with sympathy. "You need feeding up, anyway, young man. I'll make you breakfast before we wake Amy." Charles ushered them inside, down a staircase to a light-filled basement kitchen.

Marty formed an impression of large rooms decorated in cool greys and creams. He knew Angela would expect a full report.

Dee was seated at a marble-topped island unit, helping her toddler apply crayons to a colouring-in book. She immediately stood to hug Erik and Marty.

"I've promised these guys some food," Charles said.

Marty, hoping to scrounge a coffee, hadn't realised the offer of a meal extended to him. He decided a second breakfast wasn't a problem.

Dee smiled. "I do a mean avocado on toast."

"I'm thinking a full English fry-up," Charles said. "I'll cook. Can you get the drinks, Dee?" He placed three white plates next to the chrome hob before lobbing a slice of butter into a large, silvery frying pan. Into this, he crammed six bacon rashers, half a dozen eggs and a handful of mushrooms as soon as the fat sizzled. A heavenly aroma permeated the room.

"Tea or coffee?" Dee asked.

"White or brown toast?" Charles wanted to know.

Erik seemed too weary to talk, but ate hungrily. Marty relaxed as a large mug of creamy coffee, hot buttered white toast and a platter of fried food was set before him. Charles didn't stint himself either, tucking into a plateful with them.

Dee sipped black coffee and shared a bowl of raisins with little George. "Amy really is absolutely fine, just exhausted," she said, brightly. "She stayed awake all night, waiting to make sure her friend was okay."

"Who is it?" Erik asked.

Charles and Dee exchanged glances.

"Someone called Ben," Charles said.

"I don't recognise the name." Marty recalled Amy listing the business contacts she would meet in London: this wasn't one of them.

"I don't know Ben either," Erik said.

Did his business partner know of Ben, though? The colour in Erik's face, briefly restored by the hearty meal, had drained away.

"I see." Dee's grim tone spoke for itself.

The chill of the winter rain outside seemed to cut through the cosy kitchen. When she awoke, Amy would have questions to answer.

Chapter 34.   Ben

"I'm not pressing charges," Ben said, firmly.

Kyle Lassiter, sitting on a moulded plastic chair next to the hospital bed, shook his head.

"We are," he said. "I've got your friend, Amy's, statement, and more evidence besides. There is no way we're dropping it. Jonathan's breached his parole conditions, and I want him back inside. This time, they can throw away the key."

Ben was silent. He didn't want to listen to the policeman, just sleep in his cocoon of white cotton sheets. He pressed the morphine button to release another shot of the drug through his drip.

"I know he's your brother, but you owe him nothing." Kyle emphasised the last word, his voice cold. "Help us to help you. He wanted to kill you. He murdered that cannabis farmer too. The jury may have believed his pack of lies, but we didn't. We're not looking for anyone else in connection with the crime, put it that way."

"I'm tired."

Kyle raised his eyes to the featureless white ceiling. "Have it your way. My life will be easier if you give a statement, but I can do this without you." His tone softened. "Look, just concentrate on getting better for now. Once you're off the morphine, and not stoned anymore, give me a call. You know where I am."

Ben nodded.

His scars would heal. The wounds in Jon's heart wouldn't. Why rub salt into them?

Drifting asleep, he thought of Amy, and suddenly jolted awake. He couldn't let her risk her life for him again. If he gave a statement, perhaps it would persuade Jon to plead guilty. She wouldn't need to go to court then, highlighting her existence to Jon and the rest of the Halloran clan.

He was certain, too, of one other thing: he mustn't see her anymore.

Chapter 35.   Kat

Kat checked she had Erik's spare key in her handbag, then told her
assistant that she was leaving work early. It was three o'clock, and she
wanted to reach her brother's flat in Leopold Passage before December's
dusk fell. Most such alleys in the Jewellery Quarter were private, gated
and bristling with CCTV cameras, but this was public land. Shady at the
best of times, it felt less safe after dark, a place where villains might lurk.
Indeed, Shaun Halloran had followed her there only four years before.

She'd escaped then, only for him to try again. Her lips quivered.
Somehow, whenever happiness beckoned, a Halloran turned up to ruin it.
This time, it was Ben. He'd saved her life, so she couldn't hate him, but
she wished he'd stayed well away from Amy. At last, she understood
why London had exerted a magnetic pull on her friend recently.

Kat had a bottle of vodka with her. At the small Tesco Express near
the Jewellery Quarter station, she bought chicken, cream, salad, bread
and chocolate brownies. Although she rarely bothered to cook, Kat could
do it well. Her brother deserved the effort.

The last rays of the sun lit the red brick walls of the lane as she
arrived. Kat let herself into the property, ignoring the ground floor office
where Erik often worked with freelancers renting desks from Marty. She
climbed two flights of stairs and unlocked his attic flat.

It was empty, as expected, spotlessly clean but chilly. Although Marty
had insulated the apartment when he'd refurbished the property, it had
languished unheated for almost three weeks in the middle of winter. The
cold seeped into Kat's bones. She switched on the boiler, then busied
herself in the kitchen. The meal was ready in minutes. She covered the
pan, deciding to microwave the chicken à la crème if it didn't stay warm.
Marty had estimated his arrival time at 4.30pm, but there was every
chance he'd take her brother to the pub before allowing him home.

Kat texted the businessman to remind him she'd formed a one-woman
welcoming committee. She sank into the living room's red leather sofa,
reading one of Erik's selection of modern Russian classics. That triggered
memories of his taste in music. Seeing no soundbar for her iPhone, she
turned up its tinny speaker and allowed Prokofiev's Classical Symphony
to fill the room.

Finally, she heard two sets of footsteps on the wooden stairs. Kat
opened the front door.

"That smells good. Any for me?" Marty, a cheery grin on his face, emerged on the landing with Erik's small suitcase. Erik, pale and fatigued, plodded behind him.

Kat enveloped her brother in a hug. He'd lost weight. She kissed his cheeks, while glaring at Marty.

"I guess that's a no." Marty was still jovial. "I'm sure Angela will have tea on the table when I've fought my way back through traffic. If it isn't roadworks slowing me down, it's the hordes of happy shoppers heading to Glühwein Central."

"Is the German Christmas market still on?" Erik asked. "I thought I'd missed it."

"No such luck," Marty said. "It's in full swing on New Street."

"You haven't missed the East West Bridges Christmas party either," Kat pointed out.

"No, but I will," Marty said. "Angela's taking me on a cruise around the Caribbean. Her wardrobe's crammed with new clothes. My credit card nearly melted from shock."

"See you tomorrow, Marty." Kat thought he'd grasped she didn't want him to stay, but it did no harm to state the obvious.

"Ta ra a bit." Marty finally took the hint. The door slammed behind him.

Kat turned to Erik. "Did Marty tell you I'd be here? Tea or vodka?"

"Yes, he did, and vodka, please."

"It must be bad."

"Oh, it is." Erik's expression was bleak. "Our mother's gone to the firing squad, I've festered in the grey box for a fortnight, and I come out to find my girlfriend's two-timing me. Merry Christmas."

Kat retrieved two shot glasses from the kitchen, and filled them with Starshine.

"Cheers, down in one," she said.

Erik needed no encouragement. He gulped the warming spirit swiftly. "More, please."

Kat obliged. She needed alcohol herself to process the news of her mother's death. While not entirely unforeseen, it had shaken her. Joyful childhood memories sneaked into her head, unbidden. She stared at Erik's graduation photograph on the wall: the Belovs, a happy family standing together before Marina's betrayal. Kat's lips tightened. Marina had forfeited the right to her children's love.

Kat poured a third shot for both of them. She really must warm the food through before she was too drunk. "Are you absolutely sure Amy's cheated on you?" she asked.

Privately, she conceded it didn't look good. Media reports about the break-in that led to Ben's hospitalisation spoke of Amy visiting his flat to cook a meal. Why would anyone do that unless they were close to a man: his sister, say – or his lover?

Erik sighed. "She claims she wasn't unfaithful."

"What do you think?"

"I don't know." He sat on the sofa, his head in his hands. "She's not the girl I thought I knew, the girl that I loved. Even if there was nothing physical, she got emotionally close to him – closer than she was with me."

"You don't let her get close. You've been working too hard." Alarmed at his self-pity, Kat saw it clearly: Erik, intense and consumed by his research, while Ben crept in the background, trying to steal Amy away.

"Whose side are you on?"

"I'm not taking sides. You're my brother, and I love you. Amy's my best friend. I might even owe her my life. I had no idea Jonathan Halloran wasn't still in prison. He'll be going back inside, thankfully."

"Is he a threat to you?" Erik stared at her, horrified.

"Who knows? Probably. He tried to kill his own brother, didn't he? I'm glad Amy stopped him."

Taut, and white-faced, Erik reached for the vodka bottle. "Another?"

They drank in silence, until Kat touched his arm. "I've learned that relationships don't stand still; they need effort. Tim's worth it. Isn't Amy? You love her, Erik."

Erik shook her hand away. "When I was behind bars, she was with...Ben." He could barely spit out the name.

"She turned to him because she was beside herself, worrying about you."

"If she'd cared about me, she'd have stayed away from him." Erik's tone was harsh. "I don't want to see Amy again, and I don't think you should either."

"Hello? We work together."

"Sack her, then." His eyes glittered. "Choose, Kat – it's me or Amy."

Chapter 36.   Marty

"You don't miss work, do you, Marty?" Angela, tanned and toned, gazed up at him from her sun lounger.

"Quite frankly, yes," Marty said, regarding the pristine blue pool with an emotion akin to boredom. "After a busy month of exercising, films and card games, I can't wait for a rest."

His wife had found activities to occupy every waking minute on board their sumptuous cruise ship. Mostly, this did not involve eating or drinking. Apart from Christmas Day, Angela had supervised his diet carefully. Including visits ashore, they had tried twenty restaurants, in which Marty had been permitted just one dessert. As his fellow passengers ballooned from their over-indulgence in delicious food and wine, Angela guided him to the swimming pool.

That wasn't all. Within this shiny floating skyscraper, Marty had sampled surfing, crazy golf, rock climbing and tennis. He'd rarely been so fit in his life, but there was a beer-shaped hole in it. He missed the cut and thrust of commerce, too.

If he didn't want to die of tedium, he'd have to take up golf or good works when he returned home. There was no job waiting for him. The Darria Enterprises sale had finally gone through, no doubt assuring Guy of a sizable Christmas bonus. Tim was running the vodka business, and needed to do it on his own terms.

A youthful waiter in white uniform hovered nearby, not a bead of sweat on his face despite the sizzling Caribbean sun. As a band began playing jazz nearby, Angela ordered two more slimline tonics. "Would you like gin in yours?" she asked.

"Music to my ears, bab." Whilst the lad moved out of earshot, Marty stared at his wife. She didn't look ill, so he could draw only one conclusion. "What do you want, then?"

Angela laughed, a tinkling sound. "I've changed our flights. When we dock in Miami, we'll be taking a plane to Vegas. I've booked a short break in a luxury resort. And before you say anything, it was a bargain price."

"No."

Angela was taken aback. "What do you mean, 'No'?"

"I'm not going to Las Vegas. A 'resort' is a casino, isn't it? We already visited one on the boat. I lost five hundred dollars."

"I won three hundred." Angela couldn't hide her smugness.

"That's not the point. I don't need to try another, and I'm not interested in Elvis tribute acts and ageing crooners. Or starving myself any longer. I want to go home and enjoy biscuits, beer and work again, not necessarily in that order." Marty stopped talking, aware that he was starting to rant.

"You don't need to work," Angela protested. "You've done it all your life. Now it's payback time."

"I don't want to do this for the rest of my days, either. I'll ask Tim for some consultancy." As it happened, Tim had been seeking advice two or three times a week. Whenever Marty switched on his iPad, he was pathetically excited if a message appeared from his eldest son.

Their drinks arrived.

"Cheers." Angela clinked glasses with a bright smile.

Marty enjoyed the welcome tang of gin. Had Angela permitted it, he would have bought a drinks package and boozed his way around the ship for the entire journey. The bars were well-stocked, although not with his brands. He made a note to slip that fact into a conversation with Tim.

"You mentioned Tim…" She left the sentence hanging, a wheedling note in her voice.

"Out with it."

"He'll be in Vegas too, with Kat. They're getting married there." Angela removed her oversized sunglasses, fixing him with a soulful blue gaze.

"No need to bat your lashes. I'm not cross." The gin was taking effect.

Angela's eyes sparkled with relief. Her gym-honed figure looked a million dollars in her silvery bikini. Marty regretted forbidding her to flirt with him.

"Tim's old and ugly enough to make his own decisions," Marty said. "He's been engaged for nearly two years now, so it's hardly surprising they've set a date."

He wouldn't admit it, but he was softening towards Kat. She worked hard and had a good head for business. Marty didn't blame the couple for choosing to marry in Las Vegas, either. They weren't over-burdened with money or time, and Kat had just lost her surviving parent. A traditional bash would have involved hordes of Bridges relatives on one side of the church, and Erik on the other. Where was the fun for Kat in that? This way, none of the Bridges clan would take offence. Erik would probably forgive her, too.

"They want us to be witnesses, Marty."

"Really? Don't the wedding chapels supply them alongside everything else? If they don't, I'd have expected Kat to ask Erik and Amy." He reflected. "Well, if it hadn't been for that incident in London, at any rate."

"Yes, they're in bits," Angela agreed. Sympathy suffused her features. "Now, about that. I need a favour from you."

Chapter 37.   Kat

Their plane was chasing the sun. The sky was deep pink, spreading a fiery glow over the flat land below. In the distance, a dense cluster of towers glittered rosily in the sunset's rays.

"Red sky at night, shepherd's delight," Tim said. "Our big day will be sunny."

"Does it ever rain in the desert?" Kat asked, cynically.

Tim laughed. "No, you're right, it won't. Look, we'll be landing soon. Let's have another glass of bubbly, because it will be a long evening. We have to get a marriage licence from the registry office when we hit the ground."

"Won't it be closed?" Kat asked. "It's five already."

"Angela says it stays open until midnight."

"Angela? I thought you made all the arrangements yourself."

Tim flashed her a boyish grin. "My step-mum volunteered. She has too much time on her hands." He signalled to the smiley, red-clad air hostess serving drinks nearby.

She was with them right away. "Champagne for the wedding party?" she divined, with a wink. "Don't get so hung over that you leave her standing in the chapel."

The heavens transformed from crimson to violet as they sipped their fizz. By the time the seatbelt signs were activated, the only light outside came from the moon and stars above, and the shimmer of Las Vegas below.

Kat's excitement warred with her exhaustion. They had been in the air for eleven hours. Although it was late afternoon in Las Vegas, her body clock was telling her it was midnight. She held Tim's hand as the plane descended, jolted onto the ground and decelerated with such force that she was glad of her seatbelt.

Sleepily, she staggered off the plane, hoping the luggage hadn't been lost. She was wearing jeans and trainers, having selected clothes for comfort rather than style on the journey. The days when she dressed to impress were gone, except when she was promoting Starshine vodka. Tomorrow, though, she wanted to walk down the aisle in a white dress. A few weeks before, Angela had taken her on a shopping trip to an outlet store to help her find one. The bargain they'd chosen fitted her curves well.

Kat was beginning to suspect Angela of stage-managing the event. They had devised the small guest list together. Now it appeared Tim's stepmother had hatched plans with him, too.

Luckily, the immigration queue was only thirty minutes long, and Tim found their bags as soon as they reached the carousel.

"There should be a car picking us up," he said. "Keep your eyes open."

It was a struggle, in every way. Kat felt drowsy, her footsteps leaden as they headed for the meeting point where drivers stood with placards. "Bridges/White," she read. "There."

Their chauffeur, a middle-aged man with a passing resemblance to Marty, was wearing grey slacks and a navy fleece jacket. It was the first indication that the desert city wasn't roasting in a heatwave.

Tim shook the man's hand. "Hi, I'm Tim Bridges, and this is Kat White."

"Soon to be Mrs Bridges, huh? I'm Clint, as in Eastwood, and I'm taking y'all downtown to get that all-important marriage licence. We're going straight to the Marriage Bureau on East Clark Avenue, so you'll have that piece of paper ready for tomorrow morning." His eyes flicked over both of them. "Y'all got coats in those bags? I'll wait a moment while you get them out. My Chevy's heated, but it's a cold night out there."

Once they left the heated terminal, Kat realised a January night in Las Vegas was little warmer than Birmingham. She was grateful for the heater in Clint's silver Chevrolet.

"Y'all been to Vegas before?"

"No," Kat said.

"And I'll bet you haven't been married, neither. First time for everything, huh? It's a party town, twenty-four seven. Once you've waited in line for that marriage licence, I'll drop you back at your hotel and you can hit the gaming tables."

It was the last thing Kat wanted to do. While the hotel shone like a beacon in her brain, it was simply because it promised crisp white sheets and blissful sleep. Gambling was a mug's game, anyway, as she knew from her former career.

The journey downtown took twenty minutes, a ride past endless low-rise motels, malls and restaurants. Their destination was a bland box of a building, set amid similar nondescript office blocks.

Clint parked the car right next to it. "I'll be waiting here, okay?" He glanced at his watch. "Hopefully, the line won't be too long. Maybe an hour. You guys got to practise that at the airport, right?"

Tim put an arm around Kat's waist, guiding her up a set of steps and through glass doors to a large room that reminded her of a post office. A fifty-strong queue waited to be called by a row of tellers sitting at desks. People of all ages, sizes and colours stood in their winter clothes, not all of them patiently. A sprinkling of children toddled, whined and fidgeted around their parents.

"This is it?" Kat asked, dismayed at the total absence of glamour.

"You won't be serenaded by Elvis here," Tim said, a twinkle in his eye. "Or tomorrow either."

"What music did you choose?" Kat asked.

He tapped his nose. "It's a secret, like your dress. I won't go peeking in your suitcase."

Despite the numbers ahead of them, it became clear they wouldn't be there long. The tellers were efficient, dealing with customers swiftly as if they really were taking parcels and selling stamps. It seemed like a dream, as Kat and Tim were ushered to the front. He handed over a wad of dollars, they signed a form, and then they were sent on their way.

Clint was standing outside with a cigarette when they returned. "Ready for the Strip?" he asked.

Kat nodded, too tired to speak. As the Chevrolet's engine hummed and a warm fug enveloped her, she reclined on Tim's shoulder and dozed. She woke with a start, suddenly aware of bright lights in front of her.

"We're here," Tim murmured.

This was the glitz she'd been missing. Oversized temples, towers and trees stretched for miles, neon-lit against the sky's velvet backdrop.

"I'll get your bags out of the trunk and over to the bellboy," Clint promised. "You guys check in."

Tim ushered her into the hotel lobby, a soaring space lined with cream and brown marble. The sumptuous reception area, clerks at the ready, was light years away from the tired queue downtown. They were given keys for a 'nice room with a view and a jacuzzi'.

"Fancy testing out that jacuzzi?" Tim asked, as a lift whisked them upwards.

Kat's energy levels suddenly rose.

"Only if we do it in style, with a glass of champagne."

"You're on." He kissed her, pulling away as the lift arrived at their floor.

Down the corridor, gleaming with polished stone and plush with velvet carpets, they saw the bellboy emerge from their room.

He waved. "I've lit the candles."

"Thanks." Tim, his face puzzled, handed over a few dollars as the lad held the door for them.

"This is amazing." Decorated in neutral colours, the space took Kat's breath away. Opposite, a floor to ceiling window revealed a vista of the Strip in all its brash neon glory. A sofa and chairs were arranged to benefit from the view. They were overshadowed by a super-sized bed, covers turned down and scattered with rose petals.

"Where's the jacuzzi?" He led her into the huge white bathroom, where a sunken circular jacuzzi was surrounded by flickering tea lights.

"Wow."

"The champagne can wait." Tim fiddled with the tap until warm water gushed into the bath. A whirlpool button sent jets swirling through the liquid. "Let's jump in."

"With clothes on?"

"They need a wash by now." He grinned.

It was his mischievous expression that persuaded her. Kat took his hand. Kicking off their shoes, they jumped in together, water splashing onto the marble floor.

"Oops." Laughing, Tim hastily threw towels at the puddles before kissing her, running his hands over her wet T-shirt.

The fabric clung to her as he caressed her curves. Kat unzipped her heavy jeans.

Tim slid a hand into her soaking knickers, quickly finding his mark. Kat writhed under his touch.

"My turn," she said, grasping his belt and unbuckling it beneath waves of sensation. She made to bend towards it.

"I've got other plans," Tim said, intercepting her with a flick of his fingers and a kiss as she shot up again. He pushed the silk of her knickers aside and slipped gently into her. They made rhythmic waves with their bodies, until the final thrust slapped water over the sides of the jacuzzi again.

Afterwards, they held each other for a long while as the water eddied around them, melded together by the warmth and bliss. Kat began to close her eyes. "I'm ready for bed," she said.

Tim kissed her gently. "You settle in there. Not a conventional wedding eve, maybe, but the best I could ever wish for."

"Just you wait until the wedding night," she promised.

He switched off the jets and they stumbled out together, nearly sliding over the wet floor. They stripped off their sodden clothes and spent several minutes mopping the spilt water with every towel they could find.

"I'll order a champagne breakfast, and we can try the double shower out tomorrow." He winked.

Kat slapped him with a towel, her laughter transforming into a yawn.

"I'm wide awake now," Tim admitted, dodging her, "but I'm taking Erik for a beer at his hotel. It's only a block away. We can't leave him by himself tonight, can we?"

"I suppose you're right." Kat pouted. "I could do with some beauty sleep and a rest from you."

A tremor of concern passed over Tim's face. "Our plan for Erik will work, won't it?"

"I'm sure it will." Kat tried to sound convincing, scurrying into the bedroom so he wouldn't notice the lie. As she lay propped up on the bed's soft white pillows, complimentary chocolates at her fingertips, she hoped her words would come true.

Chapter 38.   Marty

"Did you know this resort had a shopping arcade?" Marty asked Angela.

"I might have done," she confessed. "Listen, we've got time to kill before the wedding at three. What would you prefer – slot machines or shops?"

He felt out-manoeuvred. "You went on a spree before the cruise, then bought two more outfits on board. How can you possibly need anything?"

"Maybe a new handbag."

Marty acceded with bad grace. It would damage his wallet less than a dress or coat. He let Angela lead him to the tastefully spotlit boutiques.

Her eyes lit up. "Look, Marty, Chanel."

"You like the perfume, don't you, bab?" He occasionally bought it for Christmas. It wasn't cheap, but he hadn't needed a mortgage for it.

"The girls will be impressed when I bring this back." Angela lovingly fingered a cream and grey clutch.

An immaculately groomed salesgirl, sleek red hair in a bun, smiled at her. "A very good choice. I took delivery of this model from Paris only an hour ago, and I'm sure it will be gone by tonight. It's alligator skin, very soft, very exclusive. Open it and take a look inside."

"How much is it?" Marty asked, alarm rising as he saw none of the stock displayed price tags.

"Thirty-seven thousand dollars," Angela's new friend said.

Marty gulped. "Do you have a cheaper range?"

"This is lamb's leather, butter-soft." The salesgirl's crimson-tipped fingers handed him a similar style, in baby blue. "Four thousand dollars."

Angela was stroking the first bag, clearly obsessed. The vendor watched like a vulture. All three of them were aware that a sale would be made; the only question was the size of the damage.

"This one matches your eyes," Marty said, plastering a smile on his face. "Look in the mirror."

Angela made a show of reluctance, then did as she was bid. "You're right, boss. Thank you." She wrapped her arms around him.

"I guess I'm getting my credit card out." It was a measure of the bubble surrounding them that he was relieved to be spending four grand.

The purchase was wrapped in a smart black box decorated with a white camellia. Angela was bound to save it to show her friends.

"How about seeing if Kat wants help with her make-up? Or Amy?" Marty decided he'd had his fill of shopping. Once Angela was harmlessly occupied, he could hunt beer.

"Speak of the devil. There's Amy." Angela waved. "She hasn't seen us. You settle up, Marty, and I'll intercept her."

Clutching a cardboard bag tied with gold ribbons, Amy walked past, deep in conversation with a blonde in a pink evening dress. Amy herself was clad in jeans and a frilly top, the sort of outfit she wore to work if she didn't have meetings. She almost tripped over Angela as Marty's wife hurried from the boutique.

"Bought something nice?" Angela asked.

"A dress for this afternoon." Amy pointed to her purchase.

Marty joined them. "I bet it didn't cost as much as Angela's handbag."

"Kat and Tim are paying." Amy seemed subdued.

"It's fabulous," the blonde said, beaming. "You won't recognise her. I'm Caroleigh, the hotel's wedding planner, by the way." She gripped Marty's hand.

"Marty Bridges."

"And I'm Angela Bridges. We've been in touch by email."

Caroleigh hugged her. "Lovely to meet you all." She examined her watch. "I'll take you to beautician in an hour, Amy. Do you want to shop a little with your friends, first?"

Marty winced. "How about a coffee?" he suggested.

"Yes, please." Amy sounded relieved. "I am so jetlagged."

"I'll see you later." Caroleigh dashed away, leaving a strong scent of roses behind.

Angela peered anxiously at Amy. "Your eyes look red. Are you sure it's only jetlag?"

Amy looked away. "No," she admitted. "I heard today that Jonathan Halloran – the man I knocked out with a wine bottle – may never walk or talk again."

"And you think it's your fault?" Marty was stunned. "But you stopped him killing someone."

"He didn't deserve to be disabled," Amy said.

"No, he should have been hanged." Capital punishment had been abolished when Marty was a small child. When he thought about the Hallorans, he didn't feel the government had made the right decision.

Angela nudged him. "No more politics. We're here to celebrate a wedding."

Amy sighed.

Angela gripped her hand sympathetically. "Still not speaking to Erik?"

"Erik's not speaking to me."

"Forget the coffee," Angela said, to Marty's delight. "Amy needs something stronger. Let's find a bar."

Chapter 39.   Kat

The wedding planner's professional eyes scanned Kat from head to toe. "Just perfect. None of your English princesses could be prettier."

Kat was grateful for her support. Caroleigh, a benign whirlwind, came with the hotel's party package. Within minutes of meeting Kat for morning coffee, she had arranged hair and beauty salon sessions. Brides took priority over other guests, she told Kat.

Now Kat had been primped and pampered, Erik had joined her in a final drill for the impending ceremony. Caroleigh introduced them to the pastor, William Peters, who explained the basics before dashing away to help Tim prepare.

A bubbly dyed blonde in her forties, her full figure bursting out of a long magenta dress, Caroleigh had a gift for putting people at ease. Even Erik, usually reserved, was chatting to her.

"Tim won't believe his luck when he sees her walking down the aisle, will he?" Erik took Kat's hand. "Shall we practise again?"

"Of course." They marched the length of the antechamber together. As they passed the full-length mirror, Kat glimpsed herself, white silk sashaying. The glow on her face wasn't just make-up; excitement shone from her eyes, as pride did from Erik's. He was handsome in a charcoal suit with a red buttonhole to match her bouquet of roses, all supplied by Caroleigh.

"Good job," Caroleigh said, enthusiastically. "Now, let's see that again. Go slower, make it regal. Big smiles."

Kat's nervous grin broadened. She beamed at Caroleigh. It didn't quite remove the sick feeling in her stomach. She couldn't help remembering her bold assurance to Tim that their plan was going to work. If only she really believed it.

"Countdown minus ten," Caroleigh said. She moved a painting of a lakeside scene, to reveal a small window. "He's waiting for you. Aw, he's so cute, Kat."

"I think so too." Kat visualised Tim's blue eyes.

Caroleigh replaced the picture. "Now, it's time that bridesmaid was here. I'll just find her for you, but don't worry. A bride can be fashionably late, right?"

"Bridesmaid?" Eric asked, as Caroleigh left, heels clattering on the marble floor. "Who is it?"

"A surprise." Kat faked breeziness for his benefit. She hoped Erik wouldn't realise that his presence wasn't strictly required. Nor was that of the other guests who had travelled thousands of miles at the happy couple's request. Caroleigh would have sufficed as a witness to the event.

As it happened, she was certain Marty and Angela would stay for the service, but she couldn't be sure of Erik. To fill the edgy silence, she asked him where he'd been drinking with Tim the night before. Apparently, they'd discovered a craft beer pub. She was amazed they hadn't found Marty in it.

Caroleigh returned with the bridesmaid. Kat breathed a sigh of relief. With only the morning to do it, Caroleigh had managed to source a crimson cocktail dress to match the flowers.

Amy's coppery waves tumbled over her bare shoulders, a piquant contrast to the ruby-red garment. Her pale skin flushed when she spotted Erik.

Kat gave her no time to protest. She embraced her friend, kissing Amy's cheeks. "So glad you made it."

Amy's eyes pleaded for an explanation. "Kat, I didn't expect…"

"Nor did I." Erik bristled with anger.

Kat put a finger to her lips. "This is the happiest day of my life. Please set your differences aside for an hour. For me?"

"Fine." Erik's face was grim.

"Bless your heart," Caroleigh said to him.

Amy looked at him wistfully. It was clear the problem wasn't on her side.

"Smile, folks. It's infectious," Caroleigh commanded.

Erik made a feeble attempt.

"You could do better. Kat, can you tickle him?" Caroleigh asked.

The notion itself was enough to make Erik laugh. Amy giggled too, blushing again and catching his eye. He held her gaze.

"Countdown minus one," Caroleigh said. She opened the door to the wedding garden beyond. "Ready, Erik? You may take Kat's hand to give her away. Amy, can you walk behind them, please?"

Kat caught sight of trees and sunlight. Power chords jangled and a rock anthem began. As she recognised 'Bargain' by the Who, Kat stifled a giggle. Tim would never choose an old song like that. Angela was sending Marty a message.

Chapter 40.　Marty

"Best bargain he ever had?" Marty turned to Angela. "I thought Tim liked dance music."

"Shh." She nudged him in the ribs, and pointed, whispering, "Doesn't she look amazing?"

"Big hair. Does she think it's 'Dallas'?" He intended his voice to be low, but he could see Tim, for one, had heard him. Marty's son, standing confidently before the pastor, turned and flashed him a grin.

The young bride emerged from an avenue of trees into the wedding garden, this fantastical park somehow constructed in the middle of a five-star hotel. Her white dress fell to the floor in silky folds, dazzling in the desert sunshine. A good-looking man held her arm. Wearing a dark suit, his spiky black hair close-cropped, he appeared delighted as any father with the honour of giving his daughter away.

Marty blinked, almost convinced he was seeing Sasha Belov. This wasn't Kat's father, or his ghost, however, but her brother.

Stunning in a red outfit, Amy walked a pace behind Kat, a longing gaze fixed on Erik. Marty sensed there was still conflict between them.

Two video camera operators, youthful, bearded and besuited, darted around the edges of the garden. Their movements were reminiscent of a complicated dance: purposeful, co-ordinated and never quite colliding. Angela had told Marty she was paying for the film as a wedding present. He hoped the price tag would be cheaper than the handbag she was clasping, but he wasn't holding his breath.

By the time the music stopped, Tim and Kat were standing together in front of the pastor. Marty had been introduced to the man, but had forgotten his name already: it was either Peter Williams or William Peters. A burst of pride suddenly gripped him. His eldest son, self-assured and handsome, was marrying a beautiful and sparky woman.

"Welcome, Timothy and Katharine, to this wonderful day." The pastor, a trim, white-haired man conservatively dressed in a grey suit, was carrying a brown leather-bound book. "We're gathered in this charming setting with family and close friends, to celebrate the love that you have for each other. First, I'd like to invite Amy to read a poem that Katharine has selected."

Amy stepped forward, facing the small congregation.

"Here," William or Peter said, opening the book at a page marked with a purple satin ribbon. He handed it to her.

Amy spoke hesitantly. "Kat has asked me to read 'I carry your heart with me', by EE Cummings." She paused, her eyes flicking over Marty and settling on Erik.

Angela was rapt as Amy read the short, romantic rhyme. "Dreamy," she sniffed.

Marty had no doubt the piece had been chosen for Erik's benefit. His business partner sat, stiff and straight, watching Amy. There was no hint of emotion on his features.

The minister thanked Amy, and asked her to sit down before telling Tim and Kat to face each other and hold hands to say their vows. "Do you, Timothy Bridges, take Katharine White to be your beloved wife?"

"I do." Tim's voice was resolute.

"Do you, Katharine White, take Timothy Bridges to be your beloved husband?"

"I do."

The pastor produced a tiny, black velvet-covered box. Two white gold rings glittered inside it. He lifted out the thinner band. "Timothy, you may now place this ring on Katharine's finger. I understand it was made in the Jewellery Quarter back home in Birmingham, England."

Marty was relieved to see Erik contributing to the ripple of laughter as Tim obliged.

"And this is the moment you will express your vows to Katharine."

The groom beamed at his equally ecstatic bride. "Kat, you are my whole world. Life is never boring when you're around."

He could say that again, Marty thought.

Tim continued. "You are fun, generous, kind and gorgeous. I'd walk through fire for you. I love you and I'm proud to call you my wife."

"Now, Katharine, you may give Timothy this ring."

Kat did so. She looked at the pastor with anticipation.

"And you may express your vows."

"Tim, it's not just the rings that were made in Birmingham. Your life was forged in my adopted city as well, and I thank your father and stepmother for doing such a great job."

Surely Angela hadn't written their vows for them, too? Marty peered at his wife. She gave every impression of astonishment and delight. Perhaps Caroleigh was responsible for the sugary language. The wedding planner, seated next to Amy, was hanging on every word. Clothed in a bright pink evening gown that could have graced a black-tie event, she clearly didn't believe in blending into the background.

Kat finished simply with, "I love you madly, Tim, and always will."

The pastor spoke. "It is with great joy that I pronounce you husband and wife. You may seal your vows with a kiss. Congratulations to you."

Tim enfolded Kat in his arms. Their passion was evident as they did his bidding.

Angela clapped her hands.

"You may yell, cheer and punch the air," the minister told the onlookers.

"Yay! Whoop, whoop," Caroleigh shouted. "Don't be too British, folks."

With her encouragement, the group burst into applause.

Tim pulled away from Kat, embracing each of the guests in turn. Kat did the same, bringing a cloud of perfume with her.

Marty found himself being air-kissed. He pecked his new daughter-in-law's cheek in return. "Welcome to the family, Mrs Bridges." He realised, to his surprise, that he meant it.

"Let's have a group hug," Tim announced. "Come on, Dad, Angela, Caroleigh, William, even. Yes, you too, Erik and Amy."

Erik and Amy ended up next to each other in the huddle, seemingly by accident. Marty had his suspicions.

Elbow's 'One Day Like This' blared over the sound system.

"Hold the hug until the song finishes," Tim commanded.

The giggling group separated again when the singing faded.

A waiter materialised with a tray of champagne glasses, full to the brim.

"Please have a drink while photographs are taken," Caroleigh offered.

"Then do join us for the wedding breakfast," Tim said.

Kat added, gratifyingly, "There will be cake."

"One more thing," Tim said. "Kat and I aren't going on honeymoon. Instead, we've booked a short break for Erik and Amy in Wales, as a gift to them for their friendship and support."

"This couldn't have happened without you both," Kat said.

Amy gasped. "Thank you." She flung her arms around Kat, caution stealing over her features as she peeped at the dazed-looking Erik.

"This is all rather sudden. I can't take more time off work," Erik protested.

"No problem," Marty said. "I've agreed with Davey Saxton that I'll cover for you. I'm flying back tomorrow." It suited him. The greater the distance between Angela and Las Vegas casinos, the better.

"Relax, Erik," Tim said, planting an arm around his brother-in-law's shoulder.

"I really should talk to Marty," Erik began to say.

"Try talking to Amy," Kat suggested, handing him a drink.

"Marty," Angela said firmly, "can we have some time alone, please? I need fresh air."

"But we're already in a garden," Marty said, "and there's champagne. Are you feeling all right, bab?"

She glanced at Erik and Amy.

"I see," Marty said.

"Sorry, Erik, I'm borrowing Marty for half an hour," Angela told him.

Marty allowed himself to be led away. "Tim told me about a craft beer bar," he said.

"Let's go, boss," Angela said. "You've earned it."

Chapter 41.   Ben

Ben enjoyed gaming meets in south Wales. He usually arrived around midnight on the evening before they started. At that late hour, the M4 from London flowed freely, and he could take his GTi to the ton. The venue, a huge hotel brooding like a citadel over the town of Newport, was just off the motorway.

The event that had drawn him this time was a trade fair rather than an eSports convention. Gamers were often broke in January, whereas the companies that supplied them had fresh travel budgets and staff keen to spend them. After a leisurely morning, Ben had browsed the stalls and spoken to the teams at three companies keen to employ him.

Provided he could still take part in lucrative tournaments, he'd sell his services to the highest bidder. He had Jon to consider now. His younger brother was brain damaged, his skull fractured in Amy's desperate attempt to save Ben's life. Unable to walk or speak, he needed round-the-clock support. Ben was determined to pay for the best possible care.

Late afternoon saw him relaxing in the bar with a pair of potential colleagues. They'd found a table and started on the beers.

"Hey, Ben." It was a female voice.

Ben looked up. "Brittany." What was the Hackney sixth former doing here?

She answered the unspoken question. "I'm staying at the hotel for two days as a birthday treat. It took months of saving up, but it's worth it. I'm going to do a degree in games development, and I have to find sponsorship."

Her dark, waist-length hair swung down and tickled his cheek as she stood with her buxom chest above him.

"You've come to the right place. Want to join us? We can offer you warm beer." Theo was the Vice President of Development for Star Legends, Ben's favourite game.

"Thanks. Love your accent," Brittany said, pulling up a chair.

"San Francisco." He leered at her tight T-shirt.

"Hang on. Are you old enough to drink?" Ben asked.

Brittany blushed. "As of today, I no longer need fake ID."

Theo laughed. "Great. Jamie, get some more beers on the tab."

Theo's young gopher looked askance, but went to the bar. Ben guessed their thoughts were the same: that Theo was twice Brittany's age, and being sleazy.

"How did you get on today?" Ben asked Brittany. He'd make conversation for now. Later, he'd ease her away from Theo's clutches.

"Not bad," she said. "A games company asked me to email them. I went swimming too, but the pool was full of couples, like the honeymooners over there."

She pointed to a tall young man with short, spiky black hair. He was holding hands with a slim, red-haired girl, his fond eyes fixed on hers.

Ben's reply died on his lips as he recognised Amy. "On their honeymoon? Are you sure?" he stammered.

"Probably. Who cares?" Brittany said. "So wrapped up in each other they're not bothered about embarrassing themselves."

The duo moved closer to each other and began a smooching kiss. Ben felt sick.

"She looks dangerous." Theo's predatory gaze settled on Amy's legs.

"You have no idea," Ben said.

Brittany pretended to stick two fingers down her throat. "Bit old to snog, aren't they?"

"They're happy," Ben said, almost in wonder. Wasn't that what he wanted for Amy, the least that he owed her? He should have realised he couldn't possess her. His nausea began to pass.

"Where's that beer?" Theo asked.

Ben saw that a flood of delegates had beaten Jamie to the bar. "You know what?" he said. "I'll ask Jamie to cancel mine and Brittany's. I'd forgotten the time and I promised to take her to dinner."

Theo and Brittany both stared at him.

"That's right, Brittany, isn't it?" Ben asked. He was throwing the dice now, unsure how they'd land.

It was a double six.

"Yes, thanks, Ben." Shyly, she said to Theo, "It was nice meeting you."

"Drop by our stand tomorrow," Theo said.

Ben placed a protective hand on the small of her back. "See you, Theo." There were other jobs around. When he had to, he made a tactical withdrawal in a game; he could do that in life, too.

He led her out of the bar, trying to angle himself so that Amy wouldn't see him. "What would you like to eat? There's a great steak restaurant."

Brittany's round face reddened. "I can't afford it."

"My treat."

"Thanks." She smiled. "That's really nice of you."

"You deserve it, Brittany. It's your birthday." He remembered the brownies she'd made for him. Impulsively, he added, "I'll ask the chef to make you the biggest, baddest birthday cake in Wales."

"With red dragons?"

"Sure." He hoped the hotel would rise to the occasion. "Want to play Star Legends afterwards?"

"I'd like that very much." Brittany glowed. She was pretty when she smiled.

Chapter 42.   Marty

Marty studied the man ahead of him in the taxi queue at Euston station. The loud black and white pinstriped suit, bushy ginger hair and short, rotund figure could only belong to one person. "It's Darren, isn't it?"

"Marty, my man." The Black Country accent confirmed it. Darren turned his head, revealing a drinker's red complexion and craggy nose. "What brings you to London on this fair April day?"

"I'm visiting the Bazakistan embassy."

"The trade mission party? Me too. We must have been on the same train. Nice red wine in first class. How come you got an invitation? I thought you'd retired."

"Yes, my son's in charge now, and I'm doing consultancy work for him." He also spoke better Russian and Bazaki than Tim. Kat was fluent in both, of course, but there was no chance of persuading her to go.

"Consultancy? A jolly." Darren dug him in the ribs, then realised he was at the head of the queue. "The Bazakistan embassy please: two of us."

They settled into the cab. "Got any vodka samples with you?" Darren asked.

"Swap you for a black pudding."

"Here you are." Darren reached into his briefcase, producing a vacuum-packed black arc of sausage.

Marty handed over a half bottle of Starshine. "You can drink it at the do, as well. The embassy ordered a case from us."

"Thanks. My lady wife likes making cocktails for the girls," Darren said. "No offence, but I can't see why the Bazakis want to buy your vodka. They make enough of their own, don't they?"

"Indeed, and I've often imported it. Apparently, they're interested in English artisanal products, though." Marty couldn't deny he'd been surprised to receive the embassy's invitation.

"Coals to Newcastle, then." Darren patted his case. "They don't have anything like this over in Bazakistan. The finest black pudding in the Black Country, which means it's the best in Britain."

The taxi reached the tip of Regents Park, then wiggled away from it through a web of backstreets. It came to a halt outside a grand white stucco terrace.

175

The journey was barely a mile. "I didn't know it was this close. We could have walked," Marty said, handing the driver a note. "Add a pound for yourself and give me a receipt, please."

Darren looked horrified. "Walk? Save your legs for schmoozing. Anyhow, you'll be glad of a cab back later after a few drinks."

A discreet sign in the arched doorway announced that this was the embassy of the Republic of Bazakistan. Marty retrieved the printed invitation from his pocket and rang the doorbell.

"Come in, come in." A doorman examined the gilt-edged card and ushered them both inside. Black-clad, barrel-chested and bullet-headed, he resembled a bouncer.

"Let me give you a pass, then I'll take you through." A young blonde woman, also dressed in black shirt and trousers, pinned printed badges to their lapels. She guided them across the lobby's polished marble floor. Marty noticed an ornate white moulded ceiling and a bust of the President in an alcove set into the wood-panelled wall.

Beyond, a larger room with similar décor opened out onto a terrace with a small fountain, potted box balls and child-sized statues of angels. There was a hubbub of conversation and servers slipping like shadows through the crowd with circular trays of drinks and nibbles.

"Cider from Somerset?" A youthful waiter thrust a tray at Marty.

"Any beer?" he asked.

"No, sorry." The youth inspected Marty's badge. "We have your vodka, I think."

"Bring some over here, then. We'll have these for now."

The two businessmen helped themselves to drinks.

"They should have got some decent ales in. If I'd known, I'd have suggested the Two Towers brewery sent a cask of their Birmingham Mild."

"Yes, that's a pleasant drop," Darren agreed.

A slim man in a grey suit broke away from a group to greet them. Brown curls waxed back, he had an energetic air. Marty guessed he was no more than thirty.

"Pyotr Vasiliev." He shook Marty's hand, then Darren's. "My English friends call me Pete. I'm the commercial attaché. You must try these canapés. They're made with your black pudding and Bazaki apple jam."

A platter was borne in their direction. Marty dutifully sampled a sweetmeat on a cocktail stick. The unlikely-sounding combination was more than palatable.

Another server nudged his elbow. "Do have an oyster with caviar. It's the last one."

The crustacean, generously covered with a dollop of tiny dark grey fish eggs, gleamed alone on the tray.

"Thanks. I suppose I could." Marty picked up the shell and tipped the contents into his mouth. There was a bitter tang to the salty taste. Caviar was clearly over-rated. He glugged back his cider, reaching for another glass as it was whisked past.

"Darren, one of the companies on the trade mission is very keen to talk to you. They own delicatessens and restaurants in all the cities of Bazakistan. Let me introduce you to their representative. And Marty, our ambassador's wife has asked to see you. She's over there."

Pete had bustled away with Darren before Marty saw that the woman he'd pointed out was Marina Aliyeva.

The avid discussions around him, the staff flitting through the throng and the upmarket surroundings faded into the background. Time froze as Marina made her way towards him. Jet black stilettos, matching her short dress, clattered on the hard floor.

Marty felt a tightness in his chest. Sweat cloaked his upper lip. He wondered if he was hallucinating.

Her voice was real enough. "Seen a ghost?"

He wished he had.

"I'm pleased that Erik survived the grey box, and so did I."

Evidently, like the cockroaches in Erik's cell, Marina and her ilk would always survive.

"Erik doesn't know you're alive, does he?" Blood pulsed through Marty's temples. He was suddenly sure that something more sinister than rage was affecting him.

"I'll be in touch with Erik. I'm certain that, without your influence, he'll sell that business."

"If you mean Darria Enterprises, he and I already sold it before Christmas. Get your facts right. Now, excuse me."

Taking brief satisfaction from her chagrin, Marty dashed out of the room, through the lobby and into the street. He was on British soil again.

Without any prompting, he was violently sick. His racing heart began to slow once more.

Chapter 43.   Kat

Kat sat in the S-shaped chair while Marty poured coffee. It was just like old times. Despite only working at East West Bridges for one day a week, Marty had retained his office. It was, of course, used for meetings when he wasn't on-site.

"I took Erik out to the Rose Villa last night," Marty said. "He got very, very drunk."

"I don't blame him. I would have done too, if…Never mind." Kat sighed. "He's upset, but he's going to be okay. Amy's supporting him, and so am I." Marty was too, in his own way.

"He told me you had exciting news." Marty's tone was expectant.

An unsettling suspicion bubbled to the top of Kat's mind. "Did he say what, exactly?"

"He said you'd tell me."

Upset or not, she and Erik would be having words. The last time she'd been in this situation, Marty had been unimpressed. She steeled herself.

"I'm pregnant."

"Congratulations." Marty left his seat to hug her. "Angela will be thrilled. She saved the top tier of your wedding cake, specially. It was smuggled back in her suitcase."

"Really? I had no idea." Kat was relieved that he was taking it so well.

"Yes, you serve it at the baby's christening."

"I'm not religious."

"Angela said you could have a naming ceremony. She expects you to hold a party. Probably at our place." He looked apprehensive.

"I'm the one who should be nervous. Being a parent is a big responsibility."

"Tell me about it." Marty flashed a wry grin. "You'll be fine. Don't forget, you've got the Bridges family on your side. The business will get over the hump too. We'll make this work."

"Thanks." Embarrassed, Kat extracted her hand from his grip. "Did you want to talk about vodka now?"

"I'm all ears."

She plugged a USB stick into her laptop. The screen was immediately copied to the white wall.

"This diagram is the current layout of the distillery. And this," she clicked the mouse, "is the new one."

"Same space, twice as many pipes," Marty said.

"Yes, and a larger still."

"What are you going to call it?" His question was loaded.

"The existing kit is called Sasha, after my father. So, the new still will be Big Sasha, naturally."

"How are we going to pay for it?"

"With increased production, which Tim is confident he can sell, it will pay back in three months. Here are the projections."

She clicked again.

Marty studied the figures, while Kat scrutinised him. Her father-in-law had lost weight since her wedding four months ago. He looked both relaxed and alert, a tan developing from his emerging obsession with the golf course. Now he was only a part-time consultant to the vodka and darria businesses, he had more time for hobbies.

Marty smiled. "Perfect."

"You really mean it?"

Marty chortled. "Don't look so surprised."

"Things just seem different." She finally realised what it was. "We're not arguing anymore, Marty."

"I trust you, bab." Marty's eyes twinkled. "Sasha would be proud of you. I know, because I am."

THE END

THANK YOU

Thank you for reading **The Final Trail** - I hope you enjoyed it! I'd really appreciate it if you'd tell your friends by leaving a review on Amazon, Goodreads, or your blog.

Find out more about the tension between the Bridges, Belov/White and Halloran families in the four earlier books in the series: **The Bride's Trail, The Vodka Trail, The Grass Trail** and **The Revenge Trail.**

I'd love to stay in touch with you, too. If you sign up for my newsletter at aaabbott.co.uk, I'll send you a free e-book of short stories. You'll also receive news about forthcoming books and live fiction events. I hope you can get to one; it would be wonderful to meet you.

You can also find me on Twitter (@AAAbbottStories) and Facebook.

Printed in Great Britain
by Amazon